ANARCHY IN A COLD WAR

Anarchy in a Cold War first appeared in a very limited Hooligan Press draft edition in the late 1980s. Shortly afterwards Hooligan Press, an anarcho-punk DIY publishing group, went the way of all flesh and dematerialised. In addition to non-fiction, Hooligan Press published several novels: *Doc Chaos: The Chernobyl Effect*, *Down Wind of Eden* and *The Free*; as well as the anarcho-satirical comic, *The Faction File*, and a collection of short stories, *From Beneath the Keyboard*, described by one reviewer as varying from 'the excellent to the rather embarrassing'. Hooligan Press also published a history of squatting in West Berlin, imaginatively titled *Squatting in West Berlin*. Most of the above titles are still available from various sources, and some have been translated into other languages. *Doc Chaos: The Chernobyl Effect* has recently been republished as an ebook. An internet search will reveal more.

Anarchy in a Cold War

Kurtis Sunday

Republished by Cambria Books, 2012
ISBN: 978-0-9572459-5-2

Cover photo: Tom Chektout
Back inset illustration: *Kreuzberg Café, Berlin* by Klara Meinhardt
Cover design: Cyberium, www.cyberium.co.uk

Special thanks to *Fehlfarben* and *Crass* for permission to quote their lyrics, either in the original or translated.

Hooligan Vintage

This book is dedicated to all those
who made it possible.
There is no need to name them.
They know who they are.
All characters in this book are fictitious.
Any resemblances to persons living
or dead are inevitable.
Minimal poetic licence has been taken
with historical events.

Central Europe, 1981
West Berlin was a West German enclave within East Germany. The city, like Germany itself, was divided into four sectors after the Second World War. The American, British and French sectors became West Berlin, while the Russian sector became East Berlin. The Berlin Wall surrounded the American, British and French Sectors. Legally, the four victorious powers were the sovereign authorities in the city until German reunification.

Planet Earth (already pretty fucked up), 1981

WEST BERLIN. Sun. Blue sky. As if spring's already arrived. Saturday afternoon. People are gathering. Have been for an hour, crowding round the intersection of Mehringdamn, Yorck- and Gneisenaustraße, blocking the traffic flow on the broad avenues, impatient to move, for the signal from the loudspeaker van. Nothing worse than standing around waiting for a demo to kick off.

Long hair, short hair, Punks, black leather jackets, safety pins, lilac dungarees, Palestinian scarves, striped drainpipe trousers, blue jeans, parkas, yellow wind breakers, multicoloured jumpers, painted faces, clown noses, black ski masks. Women and men with babies Amerindian style on their backs or chests, SEW (hardcore Commies), Alternative Liste, Young Socialists, photographers, the Gewerkschaft für Wissenschaft und Erzeihung (trade union), cyclists, musicians, beards, woolly caps, Mohicans, the Marxistische Gruppe (fluffy Commies) distributing leaflets, a Jesus-lookalike in long white robes, hennaed hair, Helga Goetze with her multicoloured sandwich board advocating sexual liberation. Toddlers, a video camera crew, gym shoes, a juggler tossing rainbow balls, kebabs, anti-nuke badges, Dmitri and his bottle of Schultheiß[1], Turks with leaflets about their people on

---

[1] Schultheiß beer, particular to Berlin. The Schultheiß man - a later medieval respectable citizen type - is

hunger strike in Munich, groups, loners, lovers, nearly everyone wearing some sort of symbolic and sometimes very practical scarf.

A lot of people, ten thousand perhaps. Maybe more. And others are sure to join along the route. Multiply the official figure the police will give afterwards by two: that might give some sort of idea of how many there really are.

And down the back streets and almost out of view: the Bullen.[2] Paramilitary olive-green uniforms, perspex shields, white helmets, new-model green-white and old-model navy blue police transits parked in rows, young closely shaved faces under clipped-up plastic visors, black boots and black batons being played with casually. And here and there the peaked cap of authority.

Some Punks, bottles of Schultheiß in hand, have climbed onto the roof of the mobile Imbiß, which is doing a brisk trade in fried sausages soaked in curried Ketchup and salty pommes frites.[3]

An incomprehensible crackly voice suddenly booms from the loudspeaker van. People turn to each other. Are they starting? No. Not yet. It's something about having to hang around for another five minutes and would people please let the loudspeaker van through to the front.

one, two, three ...

The chant starts somewhere and is immediately taken up:

---

on advertising billboards all around the city.

[2] Bullen - bulls - German for police, not particular derogatory, English equivalent would be 'cops'.

[3] Imbiß - kiosk, in this case a mobile van selling mainly curried sausages, small hamburger-like balls of meat called Bouletten, pommes frites (chips topped with either tomato sauce or mayonnaise), potato salad, beer and coffee. In parts of the city there is one on nearly every street corner.

free the prisoners!

That's the signal. A cheer spreads through the crowd.
The voice on the loudspeaker takes up the chant.
The crowd roars louder.

free the prisoners!

Out of sight, the Bullen, the representatives of those for whom the chant is meant, silently begin their preparations.
The music starts: the familiar desperate beat of *Fehlfarben*.

history is being made
es geht voran! [4]

The sound pulsates through the crowd. Bodies vibrate. Heads and feet beat it out. Some dance.

space labs are falling on islands
forgetfulness is spreading
es geht voran!

The vanguard starts pushing the loudspeaker van towards Yorckstraße.
People follow it. Faces light up.

mountains are exploding
the president is guilty

The Punks on top of the Imbiß cheer.
Dmitri takes a slug from his bottle of Schultheiß.

es geht voran!

Black flags, red flags, yellow flags, lilac flags flutter in the February wind. The banners rise. Banners with paintings on them, the red banners of the SEW with their yellow socialist-realist block lettering, and a banner the width of the street at the front announcing that that The

[4] es geht voran - things are moving (ahead), approximately.

Berlin Mob is on the move.

grey b-film heroes
are about to rule the world
es geht voran!
es geht voran!
history is being made
es geht voran!

The trees on both sides and in the middle of Yorckstraße are winter bare. A guy playing a full-sized Orange Order drum strapped across his beer belly dances through the crowd.

Two women, squatter and feminist symbols finger-painted onto their whitened cheeks, are holding up a banner: Wenn Bullen prügeln, kriegen Steine Flügel![5] Cobblestones with wings fly in and out of the Punky red and black lettering.

People hang from lamp-posts and perch on pedestrian barriers trying to get a better view. Cameras click, catching the colour and music in silent black and white. There are still people at the back who haven't started moving yet.

The police transit leading the demonstration, a safe distance ahead of it, approaches the railway bridges that crisscross the avenue. Just before it passes under the first bridge the people pushing the loudspeaker van break into a trot, and start gaining on the transit. But after a warning to the driver from the helmeted Bulle riding shotgun at the open back doors, the transit accelerates and regains the gap lost in seconds.

Stage one accomplished.

The first row of demonstrators have stopped, are waiting for the gap between them and the loudspeaker van to widen again.

---

[5] Translation: when cops apply undue force, cobblestones grow wings - or something like that.

There's a moment of silent tension - despite the music. Then suddenly there's a roar and the demonstrators charge. Wild screams of joy echo and amplify into a barrage under the cast-iron bridges. The demonstrators catch up with the loudspeaker van and stop.

But behind them another gap has opened. And another human wave waits. Then it too roars and charges under the bridges.

This happens again and again, waves of demonstrators ritually throwing themselves forward, screaming, running, proclaiming animal joy. The street is theirs now.

The anti-socials attack the walls with spray cans:

be realistic, demand the impossible

power to the imagination

no power for nobody

legal - illegal - scheißegal [6]

we are the people our parents warned us about

kein gott! kein staat! kein vaterland! [7]

A theatre group who look conspicuous, pretending to look inconspicuous, in the beloved trench coats, trilbies and dark glasses of secret policemen everywhere, huddles together beside a traffic light. The women have painted marker-black moustaches on their upper lips. One has a camera, another a pair of binoculars. The other three leer through holes in the newspapers they are supposed to be reading. Cheers and fake jeers are hurled at them from the crowd. A comic-book 'terrorist', in black hat and black cape, suddenly appears and runs screaming at them. He has something in his hand. He throws it at them. But the black sponge-cum-cobblestone yoyos back to him on its string and he smiles

---

[6] Pretty much means 'legal, illegal, we don't give a shit'

[7] no god! no state! no fatherland!

and bows to the crowd for his applause.

The first of the squatted houses comes into sight. Banners hang from its balconies. The facade at street level has been given a quick coat of pink and blue paint and graffitied. At two upper-storey windows large speakers blare out the delicious sound of *The Clash. London Calling.* The squatters on the balconies make clenched-fist salutes and wave a large black flag.

"Golzstraße 30!" the loudspeaker van announces.

The crowd cheers.

Then suddenly, more angry electric guitars and raging drums. It's *Crass.*

they've got a bomb, they've got a bomb
twenty odd years ... waiting for the flash...

There are some new apartment blocks on the other side of the street. People watch from their balconies, like spectators at a circus.

... four minute warning ...

The demo turns into Potsdamer Straße. The music is now Latin American. Last year Nicaragua was liberated. In El Salvador, Guatemala, Chile the fight goes on. The sound of the pan flutes is haunting. One can almost smell the pure air of the Andes and sense the spirit of the Incan panther.

Out of sight and out of mind the Bullen follow the parade, shrink-wrapped in their sense of duty and preparedness.

Here there are other spectators. A few prozis on day shift - this is their manor.[8] Turkish men outside kebab takeaways and Turkish cafés, good humoured bewilderment on their Southern Gastarbeiter faces.[9] People

---

[8] Prozis - prostitutes.

[9] Gastarbeiter - migrant worker, literally 'guest worker'.

drop into the Turkish places to empty their bladders. There might be trouble if they went into German ones. In the side streets traffic police direct traffic away, alone and in white coats they enjoy non-combatant status.

The Sanis, the demonstrators' Red Cross, are spread among the crowd. The red crosses, cumulating in clenched fists, on their helmets, bags and armbands are reminders of what can happen. But the buzz is too good to worry about that now. It's more like a carnival than a demonstration. Even some of the people looking down from their windows along the route seem to be enjoying it. Every now and then individuals from the crowd shout up and ask them to come down and join in. Most remain stone-faced, bewildered and weary - but some wave. Now and again there are bangs and puffs of smoke. The remnants of New Year's Eve fire-crackers. They leave an ominous whiff of gunpowder in the February air.

Some of the old hotels on Potsdamer Straße - upper-class brothels during the Kaiserzeit - have been turned into hostels for Third World asylum seekers.[10] Lots of Tamils these days. They stand in groups at the windows of the four storey buildings, their brown faces smiling, some waving, some brandishing clenched fists.

The crowd takes up an old war cry.

long-live-inter-national-solid-arity!

And on it goes, the mass of colour moving to the music, winding its way through the streets, filling them, slogans and repetitive beats echoing up between the houses. A beer-sodden ur-mensch at a balcony shakes his fist and screams

[10] Kaiserzeit - the time of the Kaisers, the last German Emperor abdicated in 1918.

a primal scream down at the mob.[11]

After they pass U-Bahn Kleistpark underground train station the stopping and charging starts off again.

es geht voran!

The demo passes a peepshow. A group of women, their scarves now suddenly masks, start digging up cobblestones from the pavement with keys. Seconds later - amid the clowns and painted faces and es-geht-voran - there's the sudden clatter of the peepshow's blacked-out front window being smashed. The crowd cheers. A white-coated traffic policeman opposite sees it. But his job is directing traffic. A brass band reaches the spot, stops and plays a tune amid the shards of broken glass.

Further back another van is being pushed along. On top of it, in a wooden cage, a building speculator in top hat and tails rages at the mob and bemused onlookers. The music plays on. *The Clash* again. *The Guns of Brixton*.

Elsewhere the 'terrorist' is at work again. He homes in on a respectable looking middle-aged couple on the pavement and runs raving at them, looking like a revolutionary ghoul straight from the pages of a Springer Press rag. He throws the cobblestone. They laugh when it turns into a sponge. Relieved.

Down Martin-Luther-Straße and onto John-F-Kennedy-Platz to Rathaus Schöneberg, the seat of the Senate, the city government, the destination. A pedestrian barrier has been erected in front of the nondescript town hall. A few Bullen in riot gear patrol behind it. A TV crew moves freely among them. But reinforcements are not far away. Rows of transits line the two narrow streets at the sides of

[11] ur-mensch, from the German 'Urmensch', meaning original (Ur) human (Mensch), cave-man type.

the building.

From a top window of the Rathaus a figure points a tripod-mounted camera down into the crowded square. Another with binoculars sweeps the mass of faces. The watchers are not from the television. Orwell-lite.

As the square fills things quiet down. The music from the loudspeaker van is regularly interrupted to ask people to move to the other end and make room for those still arriving down Martin-Luther-Straße. There is a distinct feeling of what now?

A half-hearted attempt is made to move the barrier back but a group of Bullen casually steps forward and just moves it back into place again, meeting no more resistance than a long loud roar from the crowd. But, off to the side, some hardcores are being more resolute about moving the barriers. The large wooden fake medieval doors of the Rathaus open and two files of Bullen in full riot gear pour out and immediately take up positions all along the front of the building. More boos and catcalls. More people crowd onto the already crowded square.

The music is interrupted again. This time to ask people not to let themselves be provoked. It sounds more than a bit lame. The brass band plays on.

For a minute or two things cool down.

Then a hardcore lobs a Schultheiß bottle – an empty one. It hits one of the TV crew behind the barrier. Blood pours down his face. Two paramedics walk him to an ambulance.

The back doors of the police transits at the side of the building open in unison and more Bullen pour out. They line up into marching formation, helmet visors down, shields and batons at the ready, latter-day legionaries. Another barrage of boos and catcalls. The latter-day legionaries start to march forward towards the barrier.

left right! left right!

The crowd chants derisively, half-jeering, half-defiantly.

left right! left right!

Louder and louder.
The green and white column keeps moving.
It's not clear what it intends to do.

left right! left right!

Unexpectedly two Bullen behind the barrier open it at a safe spot and let the marching column in to line up in front of the Rathaus. There's maybe a hundred of them.
The tension dissipates.
The three paint bombs that fly over the heads of the crowd towards the police ranks are like an afterthought. Two of them bounce pointlessly on the asphalt, not even bursting. But the third splatters bright liquid yellow over one of the olive-green paramilitary uniforms.
The sun is low in the sky now and the February chill is creeping back. But when the Latin American music starts up again some of the previous carnival atmosphere returns. Two woman in a black leather jackets climb onto the roof of the loudspeaker van. Both have bundles of red leaflets stating the demands of the demonstration - an amnesty and an immediate stop to evictions. They begin scattering them over the heads of the crowd. The wind catches them and whips them upwards towards the sky. Up and up, fluttering over the ranks of the Bullen. They begin throwing more. Another woman climbs onto the van and more and more of the poppy-red sheets of paper float upwards, filling the air, up and up, swirling over the clock tower of the Rathaus.

Their defiance of gravity is like an omen, an auspicious one. The crowd cheers their upward flight towards the gods. It is the last high moment of it all. Then the speeches begin.

2

A knock at the door.

Our Hero isn't expecting anyone.

It's Heidi from upstairs. Once had a cup of coffee in her place. Not his type. Too clean living perhaps.

"Do you mind if someone squats the empty apartments in the front house?" she says.

"Shit! No!"

A few seconds later she's gone.

She had been uncertain as to what his reaction would be. He really didn't have a clue what kind of an impression he made. Probably didn't bear thinking about. He puts on his layers of winter clobber. Walking down to *Godot* for a drinking session he barely notices the cold.[12]

Tina feels she has to tell someone. She speaks to Antonia.

"I've decided to take a long break from uni," she says.

The kitchen of the shared apartment in Schöneberg is warm and tidy. Bottles of herbs, sleeves of garlic, jars of muesli and wholefoods on wooden shelves. Antonia is making tea.

"I thought you liked it."

"I've had second thoughts."

"Go on."

"I suppose I felt it was all unreal ... academic. Missing a

[12] The squatted 'houses' in Berlin were very large apartment blocks, not like the smaller two-up two-down houses which were squatted in Britain, mainly in London, at the time.

few semesters can hardly do me any harm. But I really want to stop for a while and see what happens."

Antonia helps herself to some tobacco.

"You don't seem over the moon about it," she says

"No?"

"Not really."

"Just a bit apprehensive. Being suddenly landed with so much free time is quite dizzying." She lit her roll-up. "No. I'm not apprehensive, damn it. I want to get involved in something new, something different."

"Practical politics instead of academic politics?"

"I have been doing practical things with the Tenants Union. But what is that achieving? In the long run? If there is a long run! Frustrating meetings. Giving out the paper on freezing Saturday mornings in front of the market hall. I've had little or no contact with the people there except at the most superficial level - my fault maybe. A bit like the uni, I suppose - a lot of blah blah blah."

Antonia pours the tea.

"I'm going to Brokdorf," Tina says.[13]

Kreuzberg is quiet during the Brokdorf anti-nuke demo weekend. Lots of Szene watering holes are shut.[14] Half the place seems to have gone to West Germany. It's been in the news all week. The original banning order had been overturned but then relegitimised by several courts in quick succession. The latest report puts the number of demonstrators at 100,000.

Our Hero and Big Bruno are following developments on

---

[13] Brokdorf - nuclear power station building site in West Germany.

[14] Die Szene - scene, subculture, as in 'die alternative Szene'.

the radio. Big Bruno has squatted one of the front apartments. He's called Big Bruno because he's big. He takes up space.

Our Hero asks him if he thinks there'll be aggro.

"They'll smash a few heads in - just to remind people that what they are doing is verboten no matter what the courts say."

"Bit of a fatalist, are we?"

"No amount of demonstrating is going to stop nuclear power stations. The pigs will get their way in the end. They always do."

Later, after Big Bruno has left, Our Hero opens the oven floor to put in some coal briquettes. The glowing embers remind him of some lines of a poem by Sylvia Plath. Something about the beauty of fire, crematoria, and smoke rising from chimneys over Poland.

He goes back to the draft of the SF story on his cluttered desk.

Tina rings Antonia from the phone box on Chamissoplatz.

"How was Brokdorf?"

"Wait on a sec, I want to light a ciggie."

"I saw the TV. Looked pretty heavy."

"It was chaos. The fucking helicopters were terrifying. They flew over the crowd, diving down over people's beads. I couldn't believe it was actually happening."

"Were many people hurt?"

"A lot. Some pretty badly - covered in blood. I've never been so frightened or seen so much ... fear. They beat up people for no reason at all. For nothing. Except being there, I suppose."

Tina hears her take a deep pull from her cigarette.

"We had to leave our cars kilometres from the place and then walk for ages though the snow. On our way to the site we were meeting people who were coming back from it. The Bullen checked us but let us through. But there was no way you could get anywhere near the site itself. Earlier some people had been talking about occupying it but it was surrounded by barbed wire, dikes, and crawling with Border Patrol and Bullen. But the helicopters were the worst. The noise they make is so fucking horrible. People were running in all directions to get away from them. There was one guy there in a wheelchair - he couldn't even run away. He had courage."

A Turkish couple, the woman in traditional dress, is waiting outside in the dark.

"Look, I'll have to hang up now, there are people waiting and it's fucking freezing out here."

"There isn't any solution, or reasonable reason for hope," Dread pronounces. They were fairly well on, sitting in *Niemandsland* under the white glare of the neon lights.[15] "When the human race allows someone like Ronnie the Clown to have the power of life and death over the whole fucking planet, how can there be? You can lob a few stones, even Molotov cocktails, but don't have any illusions about making a fuck of a difference."

He notices Horse' s glass is empty.

"Same again?"

Horse hands Dread a ten mark note. It's his turn to go to the bar.

"It's fantastic up here," Big Bruno shouts.

---

[15] *Niemandsland* - no man's land.

The early evening sun is spreading its cold light over the cold blue sky. A sea of roofs stretches to the circular horizon. The white contrail of a jet etches itself across the blue. The air is acrid from the grey smoke drifting up from tens of thousands of chimney stacks.

The others are still clambering up though the skylight.

Familiar landmarks: the slender East Berlin television tower topped by its revolving silver sphere; the glass and steel slab of the Springer Press building; the massive grey Speer-designed main terminal of USAF Tempelhof, the American military air base; and, down by the market hall, the redbrick spire of the Passionskirche.

The last of the four of them hands up a bucket of whitewash, brushes and rollers before getting up herself.

"Well, which way round will we put it?" Joschka asks.

"Does it matter?" says the woman who has come up last.

Three minutes later it's done. A big white

YANKEE GO HOME

alongside an equally large Besetzer[16] symbol:

The American pilots of the planes and helicopters that use Tempelhof will be able to see it. That's the idea.

By March there are over a 100 squatted houses in West Berlin. The *tageszeiting*, the independent leftwing daily

---

[16] Squatter.

usually just called the *taz*, starts giving the exact figure in a red box on the top corner of the front page. The number increases daily.

There's a sign graffitied on the house door:

YOU ARE NOW
LEAVING THE
AMERICAN SECTOR

The bricked-up ground-floor windows have been painted over. One with a yellow sun giving a clenched fist salute. The other with a smiling yellow house doing the same. The background to both is fresh sky blue. Click. Justine photographs the sign and the paintings.

Rudi rings the bell again. Justine had met him in the street while out on one of her photographic expeditions. They know each other slightly from when she and Rainer used to live together in Kopischestraße. He lives in a squatted house and asked her back to have a look, take some photos if she wants to. She's never been inside a squatted house before.

"Can you give us a few copies when you've developed them?" he asks as they wait. "We'd like to do a documentation sometime in the future. Show the state of the place when we first moved in and the work we've done. Before and after."

"No problem!"

A long-haired male head pops out the window directly above them, pops in, then out again and throws them down the keys.

"Catch!"

Rudi catches the bundle and opens the massive door.

"Muck, our resident hippy!" he explains.

The hallway is dark.

"We're using the ground floor as a store room. With the windows bricked-up there's not much else we can do with it. We've talked about making it a darkroom, or even a café."

She follows him up the stairs. The walls are covered in graffiti and posters.

"This is our common room."

They go in.

"We've torn down the dividing wall to make it into one big room," he explains. "We haven't gotten around to painting it yet. One of the ovens is working. The other was already smashed when we moved in."

Muck is sprawled out in an old armchair smoking, reading the latest copy of *Radikal* – a black and white photo of some American white trash toddlers smashing a Cadillac is on the cover. He gives them a cursory glance. Sunlight shines in through four large front windows. Two worn-out sofas. Cushions strewn around a low table overflowing with pamphlets, chipped mugs, empty tobacco packets and an overflowing ashtray. A doorless doorway leads off to the right.

"This used to be a kitchen," Rudi explains as they go through it. "We're turning it into a bathroom."

Two bathtubs have already been installed and connected up. The walls have been painted a watery blue, complete with Matisse bathers. Justine photographs them. Click.

"We still need to put an oven in - one that will heat water as well. We've put an ad in the *taz* for one."

The next room they go into is Heike's, he says. She senses that he does not entirely approve of Heike. It's in good condition - and in a mess: mattress, crumpled duvet, posters and newspaper cuttings pinned haphazardly to the pink walls, a rucksack, several plastic bags stuffed with dirty clothes, tops of tins that serve as ashtrays, empty wine bottles, books and comics, cassette tapes.

The communal kitchen is across the way. White walls, bare wood, potted plants and a cast-iron cooking stove. Freshly painted multicoloured wooden chairs - obviously done from leftovers - are arranged around a big wooden table. Pots, pans, cups, plates, jars of rice, beans, pasta and muesli neatly arrayed on newly built shelves.

There's a single poster above the sink, instantly recognisable from the hedgehog symbol as being from the Alternative Liste. Under the black and white photo of German troops marching through the Arc de Triomphe, the words: Better our youth occupies empty houses than other countries!

"I'll take one or two here as well."

Click. Click.

They go up the next flight of stairs.

"We have another kitchen in the back house. But it's a bit chaotic."

She's getting the feeling that Rudi has definite opinions about order and chaos.

"From here on it's mainly people's rooms."

Nobody is in. The rooms are in various conditions of repair and neglect, neatness and mess. Only two are worth photographing.

One of them is empty except for a stepladder. The floor is covered with flakes of white paint. Someone has been working on the ceiling.

"Martin's work," Rudi explains.

Part of the stucco relief has been cleaned. Patches of a baroque-style mural - or perhaps rococo, she's not quite sure of the difference - in gaudy colours and gold leaf are visible. She aims her camera at it, focuses and presses the button. Click.

"It's taken him days just to get this far. It was covered with who knows how many coats of paint. It seems that a lot of the ceilings in these old houses had murals like this on them but they were painted over at some point."

"Tastes change."

"Originally the facades on most of the pre-war houses were all stucco. And on some of the houses that had survived the bombing it was often deliberately hacked off. It had gone out of fashion, become unmodern, they said. Stucco was out, plain was suddenly in. The past was hidden behind the modernity of the Wirtschaftswunder. Out of sight. Out of mind."[17]

They continue. The house is a maze of walls removed and doorways without doors where no doorways had been before.

"Now we're in the back house," he explains.

He shows her the other kitchen he's mentioned earlier. A girl of about sixteen with pink hair, wearing black lipstick and tattered black clothes, is spreading dollops of Aldi liver sausage onto a slice of brown bread. Rudi ignores her.

They go down more stairs, pass more rooms, another bathroom. They reach the ground floor.

"This is our workshop. Where our tools are supposed to be kept. Supposed to be."

There are no windows. A naked bulb hanging from the ceiling is the only light. A collection of tools hangs on the wall behind a rough wooden bench over a row of tins filled with screws and nails. Too dark to photograph. Cold too, like most of the house.

---

[17] Wirtschaftswunder - post-war economic miracle.

They cross the courtyard and return to the warmth of the kitchen in the front house. It's no longer empty.

"I've been showing Justine around. Justine. Heike."

"I hope he hasn't been telling you about how we are all Chaoten," Heike says.[18] "Rudi's worse than that Springer rag, the *BZ*, sometimes."[19]

"Some people here are," Rudi says. "But I haven't quite decided about you yet."

"Rudi is our resident authoritarian."

Just then there's a blast, a tremor of music from somewhere. *The Dead Kennedys. California Über Alles.*

"The Punks have awoken!" Heike explains.

Afterwards, as she heads down to the U-Bahn, Justine passes the Passionskirche. A banner hangs from its bell tower:

SOLIDARITY WITH THE RAF HUNGER STRIKERS![20]

So that too is squatted.

Yet everything else is so normal: people wandering in and out of the market hall, the winos at their usual corner on the square, cars stopping at the traffic lights. Normal.

---

[18] Chaot, plural Chaoten - rioter, from 'chaos', name given by Berlin tabloid press to protestors.

[19] *BZ* - acronym for 'Berliner Zeitung' - a Springer Press newspaper.

[20] RAF - Rote Armee Fraktion, Red Army Faction.

3

March 17: the first, gestetnered issue of the *Besetzer Post* appears. It announces that 115 houses are now squatted. A week later the second issue comes out. By then it's 123.[21]

"I'd like to go over sometime," Horse says.

They are in *Spectrum*. A big place, monstrous in fact, the largest Freak watering hole around.[22] And the cheapest. Mehringhof is one of the centres of the alternative scene. The upper storeys of the building complex house a printers, a theatre, die Alternative Liste office, Netzwerk - a sort of lefty bank that funds alternative projects - and even some sort of primary school or kindergarten.

Dread smiles one of his evil smiles.

"The price for decadent Westerners the likes of us is thirty marks now. West marks. But with that you can stuff your capitalist self full of as much socialist beer and vodka as you like. It's probably the most boring country in the world. One great grey mass of sameness, with a red streak down the middle. Only a handful of bars. Hardly any restaurants. People queue up at four o'clock on Saturday afternoons to get into *the* disco. Most of the place hasn't

---

[21] gestetnered - produced on a Gestetner duplicating machine, the predecessor of the photocopier. Waxed paper stencils are cut through using a typewriter or a pen/stylus. These are then used as templates from which duplicate documents are printed. Very low cost.

[22] Freak - a scene word, taken from the English, describing anyone alternativish, hippyish, Punky, not derogatory.

seen a coat of paint since the last bash-up. You can still see the bullet holes in the walls. No drugs, peepshows, video shops or other freedom-and-democracy essentials. Not even a fucking Burger King."

"That's a fairly superficial analysis."

"Okay. There are some good things about it."

"Like what?"

"They can get Western TV stations!"

"Christ, for fuck's sake, be serious!"

"Okay. There's no unemployment. And the only Ausländer are Russkis."

Outside the U-Bahn carriage windows Kreuzberg 36 passes by. Modern post-World War Two apartment blocks on one side, pre-World War One tenements on the other. This section of the U-Bahn runs above the street. It's dubbed the Istanbul Express by Berliners because of the number of Turks who live here. Tina is browsing through the current issue of *Spiegel* - the cover story is on the failing fortunes of the SPD and associated building scandals.[23] The party has administered the city since the war. Berlin thrives on its building scandals. She catches a glimpse of the Wall to the north. A divided city, like Germany, like the world itself. She's from a Catholic village in prosperous Baden-Württemberg.

Until 1871 the city had been the Prussian capital. Small. Spartan. Neo-classical. Militaristic. A barrack city. Engravings in old history books come to mind: officers on horseback, handlebar moustaches, epaulets, puffs of smoke from cannons. The battle of this and the battle of that at

[23] SPD - Sozialdemokratische Partei Deutschlands.

which General, Prince, Duke so-and-so is mortally wounded. Honour. Fatherland. Glory. Blood and iron.

Then, in 1871, victory in the Franco-Prussian War and Berlin becomes the capital of the new nation, the new Reich. And with the help of French 'reparations' it booms. Twenty years later it's one of the largest cities in the world. The centre of an empire. 600 km from Königsberg, now Kaliningrad, then on the eastern border with Russia, and 600 km from France.

The tenements in Kreuzberg, and in Prenzlauer Berg on the Other Side, were built in those first twenty years of the Reich. Tens of thousands of Polish and East Prussian peasants flowed into the expanding city on the new railroads in search of work and found it. Many Berliners still have the Polish 'ski' at the ends of their names. In 1900 maybe ten or twenty percent of the population are non-German speaking. A bit like with the Turks today. The tenements, the Mietskaserne, a suitably militaristic word, go up to house them. Are put up! Block by block. The plan is simple, thoroughly implemented, and economic.[24]

The front houses sport stucco facades. The streets are gaslit. Shops on the ground floors. The upper apartments, spacious, with balconies, inside bathrooms and double windows to keep out the winter that blows in on the wind from the endless Russian steppes, are for the civil servants, the officers, the new middle class. The back houses - one, two, sometimes three and sometimes even more, jammed so closely together that the sunlight never reaches the yards between them - with their cramped apartments and shared toilets in the stairwells house the masses, das Proletariat. The word conjures up a diet of bread and potatoes, rags

[24] Mietskaserne - tenements, literally 'rent barracks'.

rather than clothes, dying old young, families crowded half a dozen to a room. The back houses also house the twelve-hour-day small factories and workshops in which many of them worked. Pigs and even cows were kept in some of the cellars. Proletarian sweat builds the Kaiser's Reich. Proletarian blood oils its military machine. They are the masses of the KPD[25] and the early SPD who turn out to fight the Wehrmacht when it tries to artillery the Marines out of the Kaiser's palace during the Revolution in 1919.

And what's left of them now? The Klauses? The Marias? The Günters? The Heikes? Some drawings by Käthe Kollwitz who knew their pain and struggle and anonymous heroism. And some from Zille who knew their lusts and loves, their rare outings to the lakes and their black vulgar humour.

Our Hero finds a leaflet in the letter box. It looks official, it has the West Berlin coat of arms on it:

> West Berlin Civil Defence Office
> Rathaus Schöneberg
> 23 March 1981
>
> For the attention of head of household
>
> Re: Allocation of places in West Berlin anti-nuclear bunkers to civilians.
>
> As part of our efforts to protect the civil population in the unlikely case of a nuclear exchange the West Berlin Civil Defence Office is in the process of allocating access to the city's available anti-nuclear bunkers. Places are being allocated on a priority basis - first to essential personnel such as members of the city government, the civil service and police and fire department. Regrettably, the

[25] KPS - Kommunistische Partei Deutschlands.

places available to the general population are insufficient to accommodate the entire population of the city. So, after much deliberation at the highest levels of the Civil Defence Office, it has been decided that the fairest method of allocating places to civilians is to award each household the right to nominate one household member for a place in a bunker (see form on the back of this letter). However, because current bunker capacity is also not sufficient to allocate a place to all city households, it has been further decided, as provided for under Paragraph 34, Subsection c, of the Law for the Protection of the Civilian Population During Wartime (Federal Law 3478), that an official lottery will be held to select those eligible for a place in the event of a nuclear exchange.

Completed forms (to be filled out, signed and dated by heads of households) need to be submitted by 1 June 1981 and returned to this office before close of business on that day. Registered post is recommended as the West Berlin Civil Defence Office cannot take any responsibility for forms lost in the post or otherwise mislaid/damaged.

Yours respectfully,
Helmut Müller
Assistant Bunker Allocations Officer
West Berlin Civil Defence Office

It takes Our Hero a moment to realise that somebody is taking the piss. They must have put one in every letter box on the street.

The demonstration turns into Gneisenaustraße. A few hundred people. Leather jackets, masks, Palestinian scarves, parkas, arm in arm, angry, shouting.

aufruhr! widerstand!
aufruhr! widerstand! [26]

The world, going home through the electrically lit dusk, glimpses a mob through car windscreens. Insanity. Chaoten. Raw hate in their slogans, out to smash, taking to the streets to terrorise at night. Nothing safe from them.

one, two, three, let the prisoners free!
kein gott! kein staat! kein vaterland!

Let who free? Law breakers? Stone throwers? Spoilt rabble! Should be all locked up! Covering their faces like terrorists! Supporting terrorists too - and murderers and kidnappers and hijackers! Smashing shop windows, burning people's cars, attacking policemen! Senseless! As senseless as the nonsense about imperialism and freedom they daub all over the place! Dangerous fanatics! Thank God for the police at times like this!

Who are escorting them, in contact with Zentrale. Side streets are cordoned off to make sure the unregistered demonstration keeps to a certain route and remains under control. A riot squad waits on Zossener Straße, twenty-four men in riot gear, like a Roman phalanx. The angry mass of scarves and leather jackets hisses at them as they pass. Something glides though the air. A policeman collapses to the ground.

The bastards! They'll fucking pay for this!

"We have been attacked. We are taking defensive action. Can you send assistance to Zossener-Gneisenaustraße! Out!"

"Zentrale here! Understood! Assistance arriving! Out!"

Achtung, hier spricht die Polizei!

---

[26] riot! resist!

You are taking part in an illegal gathering!
You are requested to disperse!
Achtung, hier spricht die Polizei! You are ...

The phalanx charges. As fast as lightning in slow motion. The crowd scatters.

Run! Run! Run!

Christ! One of them's behind me! Too many people in front of me! Swish! Something's happened! He's hit me! And swish again! My head! My eyes! I can't see!

"GET OFF THE FUCKING STREET!"

Skull nothing but agony! Warm liquid in my eyes! Blood! Mine! That's the road careering up to hit me!

The bastards! The scum of the earth! Beat the shit, out of them! It's all they understand!

"Zentrale, C2 and C5 already engaged! Out!"

"Understood, C2! More assistance on the way! Out!"

The bells of the Passionskirche begin to ring.

Demonstrators jump into doorways for safety, realising too late that they are trapped there as two or three policeman lay into them. A young woman lies on the ground, bleeding through her long blond hair from skull wounds, eyes numb.

It is over almost before it begins. For the Bullen, coming from several sides and at close quarters, with few bystanders and easily identifiable targets, it has been a bit of a walkover - a turkey shoot, as they say.

The ambulances begin to arrive.

"Zentrale! Illegal gathering dispersed. We are securing the area. Out!"

Crackle.

"Zentrale, do you receive us?"

The Bullen regroup and take up positions at the intersections that crisscross Gneisenaustraße to make sure that no new crowds gather to disrupt the flow of homeward bound traffic. The routed demonstrators have retreated down the side streets. The badly wounded are being taken to hospital in ambulances and in the cars of sympathetic passers-by. The bells of the Passionskirche are still ringing. The dusk has turned to darkness.

The guy who sells the *taz* comes into the *Godot* with the next day's edition. The smoky cramped space is packed. Standing room only. The *Slits* blare from the sound system. By the window, Dmitri, pissed as a coot, is talking to himself, raising his voice every now and again, raving on about Bullen, Nazis and pigs. Through the same window Our Hero sees a police transit drive by, slowing down as it passes the squatters' bar two doors up.

Reich buys a *taz* and reads it aloud. Fraenkelufer 46, 48 and 50 evicted in the early hours of the morning. 2,000 riot police on duty throughout the day. 100 injured. 15 arrests. 4 still in custody. Brutal baton charge on the Gneisenaustraße of a spontaneous demonstration to protest against the evictions. A photograph taken during the eviction shows several Bullen in riot gear, one of them grabbing a young woman by the hair so another can snap a Polaroid of her for the files.

"Nothing about what started it in the Gneisenaustraße!" says Our Hero. "Stupid fucking thing to do in a situation like that - to throw a fucking stone!"

"Does it really matter?" Reich asked. "Stones are going to be thrown anyway. If not by us, then by some Zivi or provocateur."

"Zivi?" Our Hero asks.

"Plain clothes policeman," Reich explains.

Tina is silent. She'd come out of the U-Bahn just after it

happened and helped pick up some woman from a doorway and walk her to an ambulance. Shutting out images of blood, darkness and flashing blue lights from her mind, she begins to listen to them again. Their words, with her memory fresh, seem so much waffle.

"The demo to Rathaus Schöneberg was positive," Our Hero says.

"Depends on your point of view," says Reich. "To the so-called normal citizen any demonstration is a harbinger of chaos – the exact opposite to the reassuring ordered ranks and uniforms of a military parade. The life of the so-called normal citizen is structured around work, the family, consumption, but especially around work. When the authorities that keep these structures in place are threatened, he - or she - screams for order. Any craving for the carnival, the fiesta, the orgiastic, is submerged under the fear of losing the security of the identifiable hierarchical structure that people are dependent on."

Our Hero drinks deep from his glass.

Dmitri starts roaring at the top of his voice.

"Thugs! Pigs!"

"He's in a bad way tonight!" Reich says.

"He's always in a bad way!" Tina says.

4

April 9: the *Besetzer Post* reports 134 houses squatted.

Wilde stares for the umpteenth time at the painting of the demonstration passing under the Yorkstraße bridges on his easel. He's never tried anything like it before. Until now his paintings have been of private things: portraits, familiar interiors, landscapes and cityscapes at some particularly delicate moment. This is the first time he's tried to do something charged with this kind of emotional energy. Or 'Power', as the Germans called it. The energy of the crowd, the mass, the mob. Sometimes negative, sometimes positive. The raw psychic energy of revolutions. A mass of colour exploding from the canvas, straining to burst from the confines of the paint. Normally his lines were carefully drawn, very little of colours running into each other. He had been afraid that it was too abstract, that nobody would know what it was, but people had, even before it was finished.

The kettle whistles in the kitchen.

While he waits for the filter coffee to brew he rolls a ciggie and looks out the window. Dmitri is crossing the yard to go into his place in the back house. He seems sober. Well, it is early in the day. Dmitri had once made films. They said. Had been heavily involved in '68 and all that. Now he's chaos, pissed every day, screaming at the world at the top of his voice, destroying himself.

Some rough pastel drawings of the illegal mural they are

planning lie on the floor. The group had met yesterday evening again and finally agreed on the image and the slogan. Now all they have to do is find the right wall and scrounge enough dosh together for the paint. He had long decided to stop asking himself if it would make any difference. They were doing something. They would go as far as they could.

Horse finds himself strolling in the direction of the Wall. More than the tinge of a hangover. On the way back to the apartment from the Kneipe, Dread had methodically defaced every election poster they came across with a Hitler moustache. His politics are kinda weird.[27]

The sun shines warm. Winter is over. Christ, it had been cold. The night Dread took an axe to the furniture and made firewood of if comes back to him. He shivers at the thought of it.

The Wall: every available space on the three metre high concrete thing is covered in graffiti. Some of it he understands: FREIHEIT, SCHEIßE, IMPERIALISMUS, LIEBE.[28] Most of the stuff in English is idiotic: ANDY WAS HERE, ANDY LOVES JUDY, FUCK BERLIN. Up by the Reichstag there was even supposed to be some stuff in Irish. There's a spray-painted picture of a door with the words EXIT written on it.

The city is a nuthouse. But then the whole human race is suffering from terminal insanity. Here it just all seems to come together: East and West. Communism and Capitalism, Anarchists and Bullen, Germans and Turks,

---

[27] Kneipe - bar.

[28] Freedom, shit, imperialism, love.

Amis and Russkis, Burger King and Intershop.[29]

He doesn't want the summer becoming one long pub crawl, even an al fresco one. He'd end up going to pieces, down the proverbial drain into the proverbial gutter. Dread with him all the way.

NO MERCY NO FUTURE!

True enough!

PROLETARIER ALLER LÄNDER, VEREINIGT EUCH![30]

He understands that. At least some Deutsch is sinking in.

PROLES OF ALL COUNTRIES, HURRY UP!

Should he try and get a job? Become a prole?

FUCK THE POPE!

He comes to one of the wooden viewing platforms. He climbs up.

There are houses on the Other Side, fifty yards away, across the no man's land between the two walls. He can almost see in through their windows. The buildings look as dilapidated as the ones in this part of Kreuzberg. The odd red flag hangs limply from a balcony. There's a watch-tower. The sun is reflecting in the glass of its windows and makes it impossible to see inside it properly, but he can just make out the silhouette of a border guard observing him through a pair of binoculars. Orwell-not-so-lite. Rabbits are grazing among concrete barriers and barbed wire of the so-called death strip. Two camps, two tribes -

---

[29] Amis - Americans.
Intershop - a duty-free shop, officially in East Berlin, or rather under it, which can be reached by taking the underground train to Friedrichstraße. A source of cheap cigarettes, booze, perfume and chocolates. Strictly illegal to use, but the West Berlin authorities more or less turn a blind eye.

[30] Workers of the world, unite! More literally: 'Proletarians of all countries, unite!'

and both of them willing to burn the whole fucking planet and everyone on it to a cinder if ever the twain shall meet. And the Wall itself. Such a simple thing, a wall. Good guys on this side, bad guys on that side. Good and evil. Yin and yang.

He wonders if there are Punks on the Other Side.

Easter Sunday. Warm evening air gushes in through the open roof of the Deux Chevaux as they - Our Hero, Heidi, Big Bruno at the wheel - coast down towards the Ku'damn. The chant from the dashboard cassette player – 'MDMA MDMA MDMA' - is just right. Passing the KaDeWe department store Big Bruno starts playing tour guide.

"A temple dedicated to the gods of consumption ..."

Spring is in the air again.

"... a symbol of the new post- or is it pre-war G-E-R-M-O-N-E-Y ..."

They pass the preserved bombed-out shell of the Gedächtniskirche, the old cathedral, and start down the Ku'damn, West Berlin's main shopping street, the city's pride and joy.

"Oh weh!" Big Bruno points out the smashed front window of a boutique. "Looks like we've just missed some fun."[31]

"There's another!" Heidi says.

"And another!"

Our Hero has spotted more smashed windows on the other side of the boulevard.

The usual city centre crowd, bulging with weekend tourists from Wessiland, flows to and fro on the pavements, curiously oblivious to the smashed windows.[32]

---

[31] Oh weh! - Ouch!

The lights turn green.

Big Bruno drives on slowly, whistling schadenfreude.

"And not a Bulle in sight!" he laughs.

Almost every shop window has been smashed, the only exceptions being those that have people behind them - the restaurants, the cafés, McDonalds.

"*BILD* and *BZ* are going to have a field day," Big Bruno chirps.[33]

U-Bahn station Uhlandstraße goes by.

Heidi: "Something must have happened. An eviction?"

Big Bruno: "Hardly. It's Easter weekend. Too many Bullen on holiday."

They pass Adenauerplatz, halfway along the three kilometre long Ku'damm.

Big Bruno again: "German workmanship. They've done a thorough job. "

About eighty percent of the windows will have to be replaced.

At Halensee they turn around and head back up the other side of West Berlin's pride and joy. No sign of the Bullen. Burglar alarms howl and flash in vain.

Party time. Our Hero helps himself to another one of the bottles of Schultheiß being kept cool in the half-filled bathtub.

" ... smashing up the Ku'damm," he overhears a guy say above the music as he strolls back into the main room of the prosperous shared apartment, "seems to me to be a perfectly reasonable response to someone dying on hunger

---

[32] Wessiland - Berlinerish for West Germany.

[33] BILD-Zeitung - tabloid in broadsheet format, literally 'picture paper', a Springer Press newspaper.

strike ..."

The place is filling. The party's getting under way. One guy is already drunk and crashed out in the hammock. A Punky-looking woman, a Mercedes star hanging from her neck, is rocking him to and fro.

Rita's alone at the buffet table. It's her going-away party. She's packing up, leaving. It happens regularly.

"How long you been here?"

"Five years."

A hunk in a white jacket and striped trousers appears. He and Rita plunge with Germanic enthusiasm into a hugging bout.

Our Hero moves on.

Bodies move in the dance area.

Alcohol. Sex. Excitement. Tenderness. The lack of it.

Someone taps him on the shoulder.

It's Reich, for some reason the last person he expected to meet here.

"We are going to bring out a paper too," Reich says, "a newsletter."

"We?"

"Yes, the Irren-Offensive. The Lunatics' Offensive. The Lunatics' Attack. The group's been going for a while now. People from the hospital, students and outpatients. Articles about psychiatry written mainly by patients and not by so-called experts. We're planning to have an exhibition in one of the squatted houses in Schöneberg."

"Anti-psychiatry?"

"Yes, Laing ...," Our Hero begins to say.[34]

---

[34] R. D. Laing (1927-1989), Scottish psychiatrist, critic of the psychiatry establishment. *The Politics of Experience and the Bird of Paradise* is perhaps his

But someone has changed the record. *The Sex Pistols*. Loud.

"I think I'll go dance a bit," Reich roars to make himself heard above it.

Our Hero heads back towards the Schultheiß in the bathtub.

---

best known work. Quotes: 'We live in a moment of history where change is so speeded up that we begin to see the present only when it is already disappearing' and 'Life is a sexually transmitted disease and the mortality rate is one hundred percent'.

5

April 28: the *Besetzer Post* reports 150 houses squatted.

Walpurgisnacht. Witchnight. Three thousand women take to the streets in a torch-light demo. At Hermanplatz they dance and leap over a crackling spark-spewing fire. Tina and Justine, their faces made up witchy-white, are among the dancing jumpers.

May Day morning. Checkpoint Charlie. When Mondbogen[35] – her adopted German name - reaches the sunny no man's land between the Allied and East German checkpoints she hangs banners on the railings. Military men on both sides observe her through binoculars as she takes off her clothes, garlands herself with spring flowers and dances. Her small oriental body moves gracefully, the mane of her waist-length raven-black hair swirling about her like a living cloak. She closes her eyes, obliterating the men in uniform, the guns, the barbed wire, opening herself up to the cosmic tranquillity that's there for them all if only they too would open themselves up to it. The word PEACE is written on her banners. In German, English, French and Russian.

---

[35] Mondbogen - moonbow, rainbow produced by light reflected from the moon rather than sunlight.

The sun has yet to rise above the rooftops. The street lamps are still on. The streets are empty. A clapped-out banger of an Opel stops. Four figures get out and start unloading tins of paint from the booth.

A young woman in a parka begins marking out the outlines of the painting-to-be on the large bricked-up window of the old corner shop with a stick of white chalk. The other two are already prising open the tins, stirring the paint and sorting out the brushes. Wilde, getting a small stepladder from the back seat, looks up and down the cobblestoned streets. No sign of any Bullen.

They begin, each at their pre-assigned tasks. They work fast. Perched on the stepladder Wilde sweeps on the sky-blue. Below him someone else does the grey silhouette of a city roofscape.

The mural quickly takes shape.

Black airplanes fill the sky-blue sky and black bombs pour out of them like black rain onto a city engulfed in tongues of orange and red fire. Underneath, the woman in the parka paints the slogan:

SOME THINGS ARE MORE IMPORTANT THAN PEACE!
-ALEXANDER HAIG[36]

They only allow themselves little more than a second or two of appreciation before they gather up their gear and stuff it back into the booth of the Opel. A minute later they are safely back on the main street again.

"And now for a well-deserved champagne breakfast!" the driver says, as a transit full of Bullen

---

[36] US Secretary of State under President Ronald Reagan.

passes them on the other side.
Gleeful smiles of triumph.

May 6: the *Besetzer Post* reports 167 houses squatted.

Smash! Thud! Bang! What the fucking hell?
"That's the wrong door!" Joschka shouts, visions of the Punk crowd coming back pissed and knocking up the place flashing through his sleep-fuzzed mind.
"Open up! Polizei!"
It's not the Punks.
Scheiße! A search. Another one.
Rage at the imaginary transgressions of the Punks vanishes.
"Have some patience!"
But before he can untangle himself from his sleeping bag the door is open and a helmeted shape is shining a torch in his face.
"House search. Get dressed and come with us. Bring your papers!"
Another helmeted figure - dumpier - appears.
"Get up!" he barks.
A real no-brain.
Joschka instinctively concentrates on the other one.
"What are you looking for?"
"Suspected theft of electricity and water!"
Joschka drags his clothes on, his pullover the wrong way around.
"Whose is that?" no-brain demands, the torch-beam resting on the portable TV set in the corner.
"No idea!"
"Do you have a licence for it? A receipt?"
The other one just looks more or less disinterestedly

around the place waiting for him to finish dressing.

They take him down the stairs and hand him over to two others. He prepared himself mentally for the next few hours. Finger printing? The cells?

"This way, please," one of the new escort says, leading him by the sleeve.

Once through the house door and out on the street the morning light makes him squint. There are transits and olive-green uniforms everywhere.

"Stand there!" says his captor, placing him against the wall.

There's a bluish flash.

"Dankeschön!" says a voice from the same direction.

It's only then he sees the camera.

They've just taken a Polaroid of him for the files.

"Papers!" another one demands.

He hands him the laminated card.

They were unlikely to bring them to the station if they are doing the identity checking here.

Another uniform leads him to one of the transits. Some of his housemates have already been already processed and are inside it. They exchange smiles as he climbs in.

Horse, in his underpants, answers the screeching rattle of the apartment bell. It's a Paddy.

"I'm looking for the cartoonist," Our Hero says.

"Enter, fellow son of the Gael!"

Down a dark corridor.

Dread, unshaven, is still in bed, i.e. a mattress on the floorboards.

The sun shines in through the fourth-floor balcony windows onto the mess of overflowing ashtrays, empty bottles, bits of paper, dirty tea cups and other crud. A far cry from artist's studio that Our Hero had imagined on his way across Kreuzberg.

Horse disappears into the kitchen to make tea.

Our Hero introduces himself to Dread and explains his business: the Magazine, the need for cartoons.

Dread shows Our Hero some of his oeuvres.

Some of the cartoons are on sheets of white paper but most are on torn-out copybook pages, beer mats, backs of cereal cartons, on brown wrapping paper. Most of them are rough sketches, unfinished. Our Hero laughs out loud at some of them, especially the Ronnie Raygun one.

Horse reappears with a pot of tea and three clean cups.

"Got that idea from his speech about carrying the fight for freedom and democracy into space," Dread explains.

Horse pours the tea.

"I have an idea for another one. It goes like this. Nancy and Ronnie are in bed in the White House." He mimics Reagan's drawl. "Nancy, I had a real swell dream last night. What was that, honey? I dreamt the Russkis were hamburgers and I was a microwave."

Our Hero laughs. Horse has heard it before.

"Christ," Dread says, "I still have a hangover. Is there anything left in that bottle?"

There is. A finger of vodka.

"Na zdorovje!"

He empties the bottle in one slug.

"Russian for Prost," he explains.

"You been here long?" Our Hero asks.

"Too long for my liver," Dread says. "Two years. I was in West Germany first. In some dump a few miles from Stuttgart. Working in a mine. They were recruiting in Dublin. A few of us went along. Thought I didn't stand a chance, but I was willing to try anything to get out of that kip. I thought you'd have to be well-built, muscular like. But it's all mechanised now. The Krauts didn't know what hit them. They were expecting nice quite Gastarbeiter - like the Turks. Not a shower of drunken Paddies. Most of us got fired."

"How is Dublin these days?" Our Hero asks.

"Fucked and getting fuckeder by the minute," Horse says. "Half the place is on smack. Plenty of good Lebanese around though, what with the boys in green being over there with the UN."

Our Hero laughs. Dread smiles.

"Sometimes I wonder just how serious these squatters are," Horse says at one stage.

"Christ!" Dread says. "If you don't think that throwing stones at cops and smashing bank windows isn't serious, go out and fucking do it yourself!"

Our Hero speaks: "It's people doing something. It's not just sitting around whining about the way things are. And it's more than just moving into empty houses, it's people taking responsibility for their own lives and being willing to defend that - on the streets when necessary. I see it as a kind of sanity in an insane world. Just look at all this star wars crap from Reagan. That's not just on television - it's for real."

"Go on!" Horse says.

"It's an attempt to live communally without the state and private property. Sounds like something from a pamphlet but those words do actually mean something. Just look at the wall paintings, at the demonstrations, at the music, the way people dress, and compare it to so-called normal society. It's not without pretensions or bullshit or anything else but it's alive. Its heart is in the right place. The squatters have woken this city up. Those transits you see all over the place weren't there last year. The state takes it all very seriously. At the very least it's a fistful of sand in the mega-machine."

"You know," Horse says, "if you said that in Dublin they'd think you were taking the piss."

Our Hero is not sure how that has been meant.

"At least a lot of the people I hang around with would," Horse explains. "I suppose that's what's wrong with the place. It's just that I tend to be a bit of a sceptical cynic sometimes."

"Nothing like healthy scepticism!"

"Our Hero is involved with some people who want to start a zine," Dread informs Horse.

Horse gets up and takes a pile of fanzines from the mainly comic-stocked bookshelf and drops them on the floor.

"Which just happens to be the kind of shite I'm addicted to," he says.

On May 10 elections to the West Berlin Senate are held. Contesting the elections for the first time, the Alternative Liste (AL), a broad coalition of ecologists, feminists, socialists, citizen action groups, anarchists (of a kind), radicals, gays, Turkish and other minority groups, win 13 seats with 8.5% of the vote. But the Christian Democrats (CDU), though they have not obtained an overall majority, are the new city government.

"They've painted the mural over," Wilde says.
"Who!" Joschka asks.
"The keepers of the peace! Who else?"
"Any particular colour?"
"Grey. What else! One of those Technical Service vehicles appeared a few hours after we'd done it and painted the whole thing over."
"Forlorn is the poet who is ignored by the tyrant."
"But we went back and sprayed a big stamp on it saying CENSORED. With a big stencil. Like those official stamps with the eagle on it. Weirdly enough, that's still there."

Tina and Reich are sitting in the mid-afternoon sun at one of the tables outside the *Locus* drinking cappuccinos. He thinks the election result - the Alternative Liste getting into the Senate - is a step forward. She has kicked off her sandals and is resting her bare feet on the crossbar of the table.
"I suppose so," she agrees, not very convincingly, spooning the cream from the top of her cappuccino.
On the square opposite: groups of Turkish women sit gossiping, children are playing and the winos occupying their usual corner.
"I saw Joschka the other day," Reich says.
The three of them come from the same small West German town. Though Tina only knows Joschka vaguely.
"He's been here since the beginning of the year," Reich explains. "He's refused to do any kind of

military service, even the non-combatant alternative."

Residents of Berlin are not obliged to do military service, with the result that thousands of West German conscientious objectors come to live in the city. But it means staying for five years – officially. It's a Cold War, a two-Germanies anomaly.

"Where's he living?"

"In the squat on the corner of Heim- and Willibald-Alexis-Straße."

"What are you up to these days?" he asks.

"Nothing!"

"It's very good sometimes to do nothing. Sometimes it's the best thing to do. We don't do enough of doing nothing."

"Why do you always have to do that?"

"What?"

"The psychology bit."

Reich seems to like nothing better than explaining people's own behaviour to them as if it's all just a matter of psycho-mechanics. But, on the other hand, when you really needed it, there is nobody better you can talk to. Not because of anything he might say. But because he listens.

"I'm looking for somewhere new to live," she says. "I'm sick of living on my own. But it's not easy to get into a shared place."

"You could try squatting!"

"Not sure I could live with that many other people."

Reich indicates behind her.

"We have company."

Our Hero she knows. The blondish tense-looking guy with the sheepish grin is called Horse. Irish too, but doesn't speak German.

They pull up chairs.

"We were up at the house," Our Hero says. "We've been looking at the empty apartments adjoining mine. We're thinking about squatting them, joining them together – knocking down some of the walls - and making one large space."

"You're not afraid they will throw you out if you do that?" Tina asks.

Our Hero shrugs.

"And who are your partners in crime?" Tina asks.

"Horse here for a start. But we will need more."

"What are you saying about me?" Horse asks suspiciously.

"He is saying you are going to squat a house," Reich informs him in English.

"I said I'd think about it," Horse says. "I haven't agreed to anything."

"Can I come and look sometime maybe?" Tina asks. "I'm looking for somewhere to live."

"Sure, anytime," Our Hero says. "Be glad to show you around."

Synchronicity.

6

May 14: the *Besetzer Post* reports 177 houses squatted.

Justine moves naked through the murky lake water. There's still a chill in it but the sun beats down on her wet hair and shoulders. When it becomes too shallow to swim anymore she stands up and lets gravity reclaim her body.

"How's the water?" Antonia asks, lying face down on her blue and yellow towel. The smooth white skin of her shoulders, buttocks and long hairy-calved legs are beginning to redden.

"Nirvana."

She looks over across the lake. Her mind is still uncluttered from the joint she had earlier. Above the green line of foliage on the opposite shore a jet is coming in to land at Tegel, the roar of its engines seeming to come from another part of the sky.

She rolls a cigarette.

She feels good in this world of sun and water and nude people basking in it.

Our Hero is in *Spectrum*, holding forth: "1968! Full employment, affluence, the post-war dream is coming true. Hope. Optimism. That's what the hippies were about. Flower power. Mind-expanding drugs. Faith in technology. It's the Space Age. *Major Tom to Ground Control.* Techno-faith. *2001: A Space Odyssey.* Half the human race sees the moon landing on the box. The Age of Aquarius is dawning. The Earth photo - of that nice little blue planet wrapped in fluffy cotton-wool clouds floating in the blackness of the void – is everywhere. Pan Am are flogging tickets for the first passenger flights to the fucking moon. Détente is in the air. Some people even believe that the US and the USSR will become similar, merge even, the best of both systems emerging in some sort of benign global space-age super-state. But nobody's been to the moon for donkey's years now. The Christmas tree of technology has lost its glitter. People are still dying of hunger, except you can see it on the box now. Utopia's out. Dystopia's in. Science will kill us - either through pollution or Armageddon. The arsenals are full and the Cold War is on again. There are enough bombs to blow us all apart several times over and we want more. Bright colours, flowers in your hair, a guitar on your back, a copy of *Siddhartha* or whatever it's called in your pocket and wandering off to seek enlightenment in India is out. Rags, black, safety pins and Mohawks are in. Darkness is in. NO FUTURE. The Age of Aquarius didn't happen and it ain't goin' to. Capitalism and communism have become similar - in their worse aspects. We're fucked. NO FUTURE. The species is at the end of the road. Roll on Doctor Strangelove and the mushroom clouds. Unless the aliens land. Or there's a world revolution."

"Nah, there'll be a future," Horse says.

Our Hero looks at him.

"It's just that it'll be like something out of a bad science fiction novel."

The Springer Press newspapers accuse the writers and distributors of the fake nuclear bunker letter of forgery and terrorising the population.

Joschka is with the first group to leave the house and take the U-Bahn to Winterfeldtplatz. They're wearing scarves and gym shoes - and carrying those plastic lemons with lemon juice in them, lemon juice being a pretty good antidote to tear gas. They get out at Nollendorfplatz and head down towards the square. Groups of transits are touring the area.

He feels good. Though not without fear. It's the way he usually feels before 'going into action'. Free too. He's drawing a clear line between himself and ... the system, the machine. Refusing to do military service and coming to West Berlin was also drawing a line. So was moving into the house. He is still within the law but, he sometimes wonders, for how long more.

They reach Winterfeldtplatz. A transit, its sides dented by the cobblestones of previous riots, passes between them and the multicoloured Besetzer mural on the public toilet opposite. He gives the transit the finger.

There's quite a crowd about. Most of the people are hanging around behind the barricade made from plundered building material that's been erected near the threatened house and is blocking the street from pavement to pavement. Piles of cobblestones, prised out of the pavement earlier, lie strewn about - for later.

They pass a group tearing down a Marlboro 'Freedom and Adventure' billboard and join in, helping them rip the cowboy photograph from its hoarding, carry it away and throw it onto the barricade.

He finds a familiar face, a woman - can't remember her name - from a house in Kohlfurter Straße. She's sitting on the steps of one of the houses.

"Looks like it's finally begun. Wouldn't have any baccy by any chance?"

She hands him a near empty pack.

"It's been on the cards since the CDU got in," she says. "And this is obviously the place to start. After all, it's only a stone's throw from here to the Ku'damm. No pun intended."

"What's been happening?"

"The Bullen arrived at dawn – with building workers and demolition equipment. But a lot of people had turned out. There were more here earlier. The Bullen were taken totally off guard and before they knew it that" - she indicates the barricade – "was going up. Then some AL people arrived and started talking to the owners." The house is owned by the Catholic Church. "The church people eventually agreed to postpone the evictions for another two weeks but the Bullen said they would only agree to that if the barricade came down. That's what the guy from the AL said anyway. But nobody wants to take the barricade down until the Bullen disappear from the area. So it's a sort of stalemate right now. The Bullen are just driving around the place, and the barricade is not coming down."

He sits in the cool of the doorway to smoke. The sound of *The Sex Pistols* blares from the upper windows of the threatened house. They were actually stopping an eviction. That hasn't happened before. A Punk is bashing two cobblestones against each other to the rhythm of the music. Some people are barefoot. The cogs of the machine have been brought to a halt - for the moment.

Click. Justine snaps a photo of the remnants of the 'Freedom and Adventure' billboard on the barricade. Click. This is the real thing, she thinks, up until now she has known it only at second hand, from newspaper reports, pamphlets, from tales told in Szenekneipen.[37] None of this is supposed to be happening. But neither were 1789, 1848, the Paris Commune supposed to have happened. Nor the révolutionette, May 1968.

But there is another side to all that she sees: violence. It's out there, waiting, abstract as yet, unformed, beyond the crowd, beyond the patrolling transits, beyond the physicality of what is happening around her, poised to slice into it, smashing glass and skulls.

She loads a new roll of the cheap East German film from Intershop into the camera. A ritual of her craft.

She remembers a photograph: executed communards, black and white, the contorted faces of strangers from another time, rows and rows of them in plain pine coffins.

The evening sun sets somewhere behind the streets of houses. Shadows and then darkness comes. Only a matter of time now, Joschka thinks, taking a slug of Schultheiß.

---

[37] Szenekneipe - from 'Szene' and 'Kneipe', scene bar, an 'alternative bar'.

"I'm moseying down to Winterfeldtplatz," Dread says, putting his Doc Martens on. "You comin'?"

Horse: "Naw! Don't feel like walking into something I know nothing about. But disable a few Bullen for me anyway!"

Dread has no illusions about why he is going. It's simply to work out his frustrations, as he put it in the Kneipe the other night. And maybe aim his aggression in halfway the right direction for a change, instead of at himself. And the bastards are fair game - the risk to him is far greater than it is to them.

Joschka, a cobblestone in each hand, waits in the darkness. There is a group of them. He should be tired - he's been lobbing stones at the patrolling transits for nearly half an hour - but he isn't. The animal in him is thriving on the adrenalin.

One, two, three sets of transit headlights slowly round the corner. And flashing lights. Cold bursts of neon blueness. His breath quickens behind the damp scarf that covers his face. The transit motors roar. They accelerate. A hail of cobblestones flies through the air, battering the green metallic hulk of the first one as it speeds past. A second hail hits the back door of the third one. That should make the bastards think twice about stopping and getting out.

Dread is one of the others. He wants what he likes to call 'a direct hit' - to actually hit one of the mindless fuckers, not just one of their poxy transits. But for that he'll have to wait until they stop and actually get out. He's had a few bottles of Schultheiß and few measures of schnapps.

He sees more blue flashes approaching. One, two,

three, four, five of them. Glancing back to check his escape route to the barricade, he gets into position and throws his first stone. It hits the metallic hulk of the transit amidst a hail of other stones. Brakes screech and the transits come to a sudden rocking halt, their back doors swinging open. Dread aims his second cobblestone at one of the first of the Bullen to jump out. It bounces off the guy's shield. More Bullen tumble out of the transits, half a dozen from each transit. Another hail of stones flies through the air. The street fighters turn and run towards the protection of the barricade. It just over fifty metres away but unhampered, as the Bullen are, by heavy protective gear, they reach it safely. Dread takes another stone from the pocket of his donkey jacket as he runs past some panicking drinkers outside *Slumberland* scuttling like mad into the narrow doorway of the Kneipe. He glances back. There's a lone Bulle less than twenty metres behind him. Glasses of beer from the crowd rain in the direction of Bulle and of another one following close behind him. Dread turns around. The Bulle is laying into someone curled up on the pavement with his white baseball bat-like baton. Now, now, Dread's will screams at him, now, do it now! He takes aim at the Bulle's momentarily unprotected chest and throws. The cobblestone grazes the Bulle's shield and hits him on the shoulder. He stumbles backwards - the pain contorting his face invisible behind his faceless visor. The image ingrains itself in Dread's mind's eye. He turns and runs towards the gap at the side of the barricade which at that precise moment is being engulfed in flames.

"It was fucking crazy! There was fighting all over the place. But you only saw what was going on around you," Justine tells someone later. "I was in *Slumberland.* It's a schicky-micky place. No political posters or anything like that. But still more or less on our side. The place was packed. They were doing a roaring trade. People were looking out through the plate glass windows at what was happening on Winterfeldtplatz – as if the world outside was some sort of goldfish bowl. Or the other way around? It was surreal: Bob Marley's 'stand up, stand up for your rights' playing full blast on the stereo and outside the Bullen dodging stones and beating the shit out of anyone they could catch. The barricade was in flames by then. There were also people milling around outside, drinking. Every time the Bullen stopped and jumped out of their transits there was a mad rush to get in through the door with people jettisoning their bottles and glasses by throwing them at the Bullen. They'd just manage it in a nick of time and leave the Bullen outside staring at us through the plate glass windows. People were giving them the finger and making faces at them. Some of the Bullen were tapping at the glass with their batons to say: You just wait! And all the time Bob Marley in the background singing 'stand up, stand up for your rights'. One or two people were caught outside and the Bullen gave them a right going over. Some Sanis had set up a sort of First Aid station in one corner for the injured. Some people were quite badly hurt, bleeding from the head. The *taz* reckoned that over a hundred people were injured altogether. However, once we were inside the Kneipe we were safe. The door was made of solid steel. As the night went on and the people were getting drunker and the Bullen angrier. Eventually one of them managed to wedge a baton in the door. Merde alors, was there panic then! People running all round the place, trying to get as far away from the door as possible. Luckily, I was at the end furthest away. I was going to take out my camera, but I thought better of it. Outside, about twenty of them had lined up in a row and some officer was barking an order. It must have been for them to change batons. They clipped their big wooden ones to the inside of their shields and took out their small black rubber ones, the ones they use inside. I was shitting myself. Most people were, except those that were too pissed or furious and were calling them pigs and assholes and anything else they could think of. When they burst in they were met by a hail of glasses, bottles, chairs and ashtrays, but it all just bounced off their shields and helmets. They went straight for the Sanis and a few who'd been earmarked for making faces at them through the window got belted around too. Then, screaming and shouting at us, they frogmarched us out of the place. It was easy enough for them - everybody just wanted to get out of there. Outside, they lined us up against the wall, made a few arrests, all guys, and told us to disappear. Some people did, but, most refused to go until ambulances for the injured were called."

7

"This one is easy to get into," Our Hero says to Tina, kicking the door open.

It's the usual one room and kitchen, in good nick. Basically needing only a coat of paint. He shows her the wall in the hall he intends to knock down.

"We can turn the kitchen into a bathroom eventually. The plumbing is all there. All it needs is a bathtub, a gas heater and a few days' work." One outside stairwell toilet is shared by the four apartments and that cannot be changed. "There is one other room free, but it's in the worst condition of the lot."

She had kind of hoped that Horse would be around.

"Is your friend, Horse, going to move in?" she asks.

"I'll show you the room he wants."

"And when are you going to knock down the walls?" she asks, following him out into the courtyard.

"I'd like to do it right now but Horse and I are tied up with getting the Magazine together. But if you want to move in, just go for it!"

He shows her the other apartment through the window. It consists of two rooms of about equal size. The plan is for one room to be joined to the kitchen in his apartment to form a common room - the other is the one Horse wants.

"As you can see, the windows need some panes of glass and there's a fair amount of plastering to be done."

The fourth and last apartment is full of junk. It is also the only one that cannot be connected up to the others.

"Well?" he says finally, leaning against the window sill, taking out his tobacco.

She makes a face.

"I'll go for it," she says.

June 5: the *Besetzer Post* reports 181 houses squatted.

"It was a victory," Joschka says. "We stopped an eviction."

"Caught them momentarily off guard, that's all, is more like it," Wilde replies.

Typical, Joschka thinks, stirring honey into his coffee.

"It's a mistake " Wilde goes on, "to see things too much in terms of the street or giving the Bullen a good trashing. We need wider perspectives."

"But it's the streets and direct action which is keeping the movement going."

A change of subject.

"Any new plans for wall paintings?"

"Yes, one."

They go into the studio.

As Wilde roots around behind some canvases, Joschka notices the painting of the demo going under the Yorckstraße bridges.

"That would make a good poster!" he says.

Wilde spreads a roll of brown paper out on the floor. It has a sketch for a proposed wall painting on it.

"This is still pretty rough," he explains. "These are supposed to be bubbles - glass cages. There is a person in each, alone - one with a TV set, another with a car, and so on."

"Alienation."

"And the fragile pointlessness of consumer life."

"And what is that figure there - in the background?"

"Death - with a scythe. Just about to harvest. The working title's *If you only knew what plans they have for you!* This time we want to be a bit more subtle than the last time. Might save it from being painted over as soon as it sees the light of day. Give it some time to work on brain cells."

"A grey wall with CENSORED stamped all over it works on brain cells too."

"What time is it?" Horse mutters from the couch.

"Half-past ten," Our Hero informs him, opening the windows. "It's a scorcher outside. I've been down the market getting some goodies for breaky. If you can bear to arise to face another day on planet Earth - and clear this mess up - it'll be ready in ten minutes."

The previous night's events flash through Horse's fuzzy mind. *Schelmihl*. Incessant talk about the Magazine. Tequilas, pinches of salt, slices of lemon. Vitamin C. Then back here to Our Hero's and a joint before crashing out. City birdsong drifts through the open windows. Yin to the yang of his hungover soul.

"How's the head?" Our Hero shouts from the kitchen.

"Still there!"

"Funny. I don't have any hangover at all, and that's rare. Probably to do with my state of mind while I'm drinking, I suppose."

"It's chemicals! All states of consciousness can be explained chemically. That's why people use drugs."

Horse clears the table of the previous night's mess.

Our Hero appears with the bacon, eggs and fresh white bread rolls.

"All groups, cultures, individuals can be classified by the drugs they use. Every culture is into something. The hippies were into dope and acid, the Punks are alcohol users - as well as being into smack. Gays are into poppers. The desperate housewife survives on Valium. The American Indians were into peyote ... and tobacco. The ancient Celts were off their bops on mushrooms ... and into booze. Skinheads are into speed."

They start to eat.

"And what about the staff of the White House? The Bullen?"

"Coke. Only the best for the upper two percent. The Bullen would be mainly into alcohol, but then nearly everyone in our society is. Drugs are a constant in human culture. The Second World War was run on speed. 'Just pop vun of zeese little pills, Fritz, und you vill be in Moscow before you know it.' And Vietnam was run on smack and acid. All this moralising about them is just a load of shite."

Our Hero pours cups of strong Aldi filter coffee.

"And what about this one?" he asks.

"Caffeine is really potent. It's just that we consume so much of the stuff we don't notice. Coffee houses used to be hot beds of revolution in England, and illegal at one stage, I think. Ban it and you'd have caffeine barons - and a 'war on caffeine'."

"Maybe that was because by drinking coffee instead of gin they were able to halfway engage in the mental activity called thinking," Our Hero suggests. "And it wasn't just thoughts of revolutions that were spinning around their caffeine-enhanced and nicotine-enhanced brains. The East India Company and Lloyds were also run from coffee dens. We were discussing hangovers."

"Paddy Catholic guilt sets off chemical reactions in Paddy Catholic brain experiencing alcohol deprivation."

"Guilt releases chemicals. Or chemicals induce guilt. Shouldn't it be either one or the other?"

"That's just Western dualism. Cause and effect stuff. Linear. Things happen together. Cause and effect is only an aspect of that, not the whole thing."

"Elucidate," Our Hero urges.

"Take a Western science par excellence: nuclear physics. A thing is isolated - an atom in this case - and certain things are done to it. It goes boom. Bang. Typically Western. Me-no-understand. Me-take-it-asunder. Me-make-it-go-bang."

"My name iz Wernher von Braun. I make ze rockets zhat go up. Where zee come down iz not my department."

"And from all that they form a theory about what the thing is supposed to be like inside. Not that it has an inside. And in the end what do we really know about atoms? Fuck all! Except that if you do A and B to one it goes bang! And then we put as many bangs as will fit on top of Wernher's rockets."

Our Hero rolls a ciggie, the glorious first one of the day, enjoying Horse's mishmash of bullshit and perhaps insight.

"What's today's activity schedule?" Horse asks, making an impressive impersonation of an upbeat Californian.

"Pretending to be Kurt Vonnegut for a few hours. Then to see if my unemployment money has come through at the bank."

"If you give me some of your stories, I'll have a look at them, and give you my informed literary opinion on said documents."

It's just after three in the morning. Joschka and Big Bruno, the latter doing the driving, most of the talking and choosing the tapes, are doing a night watch shift. They are leaving Kreuzberg 36 and are heading down Kopischstraße towards Chamissoplatz, passing the house known as K5.

"A nuthouse, if there ever was one," Big Bruno remarks.

They turn left onto Willibald-Alexis-Straße.

"All quiet on the Western front tonight," he goes on. "If I didn't enjoy driving and listening to music - and irregular hours - I'd never have put my name down for this."

Joschka does not quite approve of Big Bruno's flippancy. He'd put his name down out of something akin to a sense of duty ... a word hopelessly loaded with reactionary connotations.

"Yeah, I suppose it is boring," he admits.

Though several times a convoy of transits had been spotted on its way to search or evict a house – and the telephone chain had been activated. And once, supposedly, a patrol had come across a group of

Faschos about to petrol bomb a house.

Big Bruno suddenly slows the battered VW bus down.

There's a transit up ahead of them - one of the older blue ones. They can just make out its shape in the gaslight. It's stopped outside *Krautscho*, the Besetzer café a few doors down from *Godot*.

Its back doors suddenly swing open and two helmeted Bullen, shields at the ready, jump out, one of them dashing towards the café door, grabbing something and carrying it back to the transit.

"A chair!" Joschka shakes his head in disbelief. "A fucking chair! They're after taking one of the chairs left outside."

The transit speeds off into the darkness.

"City ordinance X, paragraph Y, sub-section Z, regulating the number of chairs allowed on the pavement outside cafés, Kneipen and restaurants, also specifies that without specific permission the leaving of chairs and tables out overnight is verboten. The law's the law is the law."

They turn down Heimstraße, heading towards the next Besetzer stronghold in Schöneberg.

Justine's photograph of the burning 'Freedom and Adventure' placard is in the *Besetzer Post*. She'd sent it off to them on spec.

She hands the magazine to Antonia. They are in *Slumberland*. It's half-past ten. Early yet.

Justine is drinking Weizenbier. Things are looking up. She'd gotten her first unemployment cheque the day before yesterday. And now her photograph has been published.

The Weizenbier is cool and tangy. German New Wave is coming over the stereo. The chic clientele in their chic clothes and chic hair styles are drinking their upmarket drinks. A change from the dour politicos of Kreuzberg. She's come a long way from being a secretary in a fluorescent-lit glass and aluminium office block. The train of events that brought her here drifts though her mind. A sunny day on a Camargue beach. Rainer: blond, fun-loving, sensitive, serious, speaking French with a charming German accent. Fucking under ancient Mediterranean stars. But holidays end and it's back to secretary-world and rat race. Letters. The allure of a distant city. German lessons at the Goethe Institute in Paris. And then one snowy morning, breakfasting in a café at Pont Neuf, Notre Dame visible in the distance, she makes a decision. Driving to West Germany in her Deux Chevaux. But the Teutonic knight in shining armour drinks too much. His fun-loving metamorphosed into irresponsibility, his seriousness into moroseness, his sensitivity into touchiness and jealousy. The summer magic is gone. She leaves him. He wishes her luck and means it. Months spent in rooms in various shared apartments. Surfing the waves of the sea of the world.

"This magazine has come on," Antonia says, closing it and putting it down. "From a few barely legible and badly gesternered sheets of paper stapled together, every second sentence a mindless slogan ... to nicely printed, glossy cover, informative articles."

"I fancy a Tequila," Justine suggests.

Antonia doesn't need any coaxing to join her.

8

The words on Our Hero's notepad swim in the heat and a fly crawls over the sloppily typewritten sheet of paper. Fuck, it's too hot to write. But the sun on his bare back and buttocks feels good. Further down from him, near the tall leafy trees, two women are also sun bathing in the nude. Usually in the Hasenheide, unlike at the lakes, people are a bit inhibited about stripping off. It's been a long time, too long, since he's last made love, fucked. The half-drunken one night stands since Petra, which were rare enough anyway, hardly count. Sexuality. Should be simple. But it isn't.

He allows his back to bake for a while before turning over. Hatha Yoga time. He relaxes, limb by limb, muscle by muscle, and eventually feels like lead, as if he is being pulled into the earth.

Later, smoking a roll-up, he contemplates the blue sky, the burning sphere and the green grass. There are insects everywhere. And people on rugs, children playing, Turkish women in multicoloured shawls picnicking with their toddlers.

The two Matisse-women are still there, lying motionless on their fronts. Is he ever going to get out of thinking, whenever he sees an eligible female, that she might be it, 'the one'? Pathetic really.

Tina springs to mind. He finds her physically attractive but ... the thought is somehow depressing, chasm-opening.

There's that Gastarbeiter Turkish guy again, middle-aged, moustached, in God only knows what kind of a shitty job - he'd noticed him earlier - walking past the two women, slowing down as he approaches them, staring at them, this time blatantly. What kind of a sexual world does he live in, Our Hero wonders.

"Get away, you creep!"

Angry women's voices.

"Piss off!"

And the sad figure in the shabby dark suit, out of place in sun-drenched Arcadia, begins to quickly walk away, muttering: "Excuse me! Excuse me!"

Schreiner plants the portable black and white television set in the corner of the room on a wooden box, collapses into the old armchair and prises the top off the day's second bottle of Schultheiß with his teeth.

"The opium of the people," Big Bruno says. "And cheaper than a lobotomy."

"Schultheiß?"

"No, television."

Schreiner is moving into the apartment on the second floor of Willibald-Alexis-Straße 11, squatting it. Big Bruno has helped him move his stuff in the VW from the overcrowded place in Großbeerenstraße where he'd been crashing since the Fraenkelufer eviction. He has spent the last week painting it and generally doing it up. Finally, he's moved in.

He's glad to be out of Großbeerenstraße. No group feeling. Certainly not in comparison to Fraenkelufer. He'd gotten off H there. Big Bruno had told him about this place. An apartment in a back house on its own. Lots of other apartments in the house are still empty but there's some Irish guy downstairs who's supposed to be organising some people to move into the ones down there. And there's this woman with a baby who's doing up the one opposite.

He takes a slug from his bottle. It's been thirsty work.

Big Bruno starts fiddling with the tape player.

A woman with frizzy short hair, blond, blue saucer-eyes in a round smiling face, with a baby on her back, appears in the doorway.

"Hi, I'm Kalypso," she introduces herself. "From opposite. Your new neighbour. Or will be when I move in. I've already painted the place. I hope to move my stuff in tomorrow or the day after. And this is Fröschchen." She means the baby.[38]

"Want a beer?"

"I'm breastfeeding."

"It'll help make a man of him."

"It's a her."

"Then it'll put hair on her chest."

"You win."

Schreiner opens another Schultheiß, this time with the opener he has permanently hanging from the waist of his leather trousers and hands it to her.

"So the forces of law and order made an appearance down your way yesterday," Big Bruno says out of the blue. "There was an article in the *taz*."

Kalypso's been living in the Oranienstraße in Kreuzberg 36.

"From the look of them in the photo they were big

---

[38] Fröschchen - little frog.

bastards," he adds.

"What happened?" Schreiner asks.

Kalypso gets in first.

"One of the houses was searched - by Zivis wearing ski masks and carrying those baseball-bat batons. We thought they were Faschos at first but there were uniformed Bullen there too, and when I saw them chatting away to each other it clicked. They were trying to look like what they imagine your *BILD-Zeitung* Chaot looks like. But their leather jackets were too new, and the ironed jeans were a dead give-away. Some of them even had no-brain ads on their T-shirts."

"They're all fascist pigs," Schreiner says.

"Only doing their job," Big Bruno laughs.

"Their manner was enough to make you vomit," Kalypso continues. "Disgusting. A blatant display of macho power. You could just see that they couldn't give a shit. No wonder people throw stones at them! Nothing happened though. They didn't find anything or arrest anyone."

Big Bruno is still fiddling with the tape player.

"I think I've done it," he says and suddenly a deafening roar from the speakers shakes the room. The sound of *Crass*.

middle class, working class, it's all a load of shit
middle class, working class, it's all a load of shit

Fröschchen begins to bawl.

"Did I cause that?" Big Bruno laughs, turning down the volume.

"Maybe, but she's probably hungry too."

Waiting, waiting in their silos across the world, thousands of them, their precise seductive insignia stencilled onto their smooth hulls. Buttons are pressed. Missiles glide through the sky, towards cities, carrying payloads of mega-death.

The naked force of it tears Tina from her dream. The original roar gives way to another. Thunder.

She is sweating.

If it had been she wouldn't have heard the blast anyway.

It is raining. The sound of its freshness falling on dry buildings and its splashing against the window panes is reassuring.

But it could have been.

She wonders if many have dreams like that.

Dread is suggesting they declare Kreuzberg independent: "... build a wall around it, print our own money. Machine-gun posts, barbed wire, the lot. The tourists would come in droves. Make them change their hard-earned West German marks for our own equivalent just like they do on the Other Side."

He, Horse and Our Hero are in *Spectrum* again.

"Wouldn't be that difficult. The place is half-surrounded by the Wall anyway. And think of all the cushy jobs! Embassies around the globe. The Embassy of the Anarchist Republic of Kreuzberg. I can see it inscribed on a brass plaque on some tasteful Georgian building in London. And fleets of rainbow-coloured limousines with little red and black flags fluttering on their bonnets. Our own passports - in two languages, Szenedeutsch and Turkish - black print on red pages. The possibilities are endless!"

The place is packed. Smelling of beer, sweat and smoke.

"I'd like the Jamaica posting. A veranda overlooking the beach. Pleasant sea breeze taking the worst of the heat out of the tropical evening. A joint in one hand - one from the embassy plantation natürlich - an iced rum and coke in the other. The stereo blasting out Bob Marley and on the horizon the mushroom clouds blooming. Their 'terrible beauty' being reflected on the mirror of the tropical sea."[39]

He empties his glass.

Horse takes the hint and heads to the crowded bar.

It's been a good day. They've finally settled a publication date for the Magazine.

Horse returns five minutes later with three sparkling point-four litre glasses of beer.

"To the Anarchist Republic!" he toasts. "Na zdorovje!"

Tina pedals through the quiet Saturday afternoon streets, the warm air cool on her bare legs, gliding in and out of the shadows of the trees along the glimmering polluted canal, heading in the general direction of Kreuzberg 36.

She passes the bricked-up Frankelufer houses.

She reaches Kottbusser Tor. A train screeches to a halt in the overhead U-Bahn station. A banner hangs from the walkway across Adalbertstraße. The big red words are in Turkish but she can make it out: DOWN

[39] In his poem *Easter, 1916*, about the Irish 1916 uprising in Dublin, which started on an Easter Monday, W B Yeats wrote, describing the events, 'a terrible beauty is born'.

WITH THE JUNTA! The Wall is visible at the end of the street. The Berliner Bank windows are boarded up. They've been smashed so many times they've given up replacing them.

The tourist buses don't venture this far. This is a slum, a ghetto to the average Berliner. Kebab takeaways. Turkish shops. The spicy whiff of the Orient in the air. Big Turk-driven second-hand cars. Half the graffiti and posters on house walls in an alien and incomprehensible tongue. Old men with worry beads. Women and girls wearing multicoloured head scarves. Groups of young men in blue jeans smoking Marlboros on street corners.

And alongside this, as *Fehlfarben* put it, are 'die Türken von morgen', tomorrow's Turks: the Besetzer, the youth, the losers. Defiant banners hang from the windows of the squatted houses. Groups of Punks sit on the pavement drinking cheap beer from Aldi. Up nearer the Wall, at the quieter end of the street, a group of hippyish-studenty types have set up a table and chairs in a commandeered parking space and are drinking wine from glasses and eating bread and cheese.

It's here that the Senate's regeneration policies have hit the hardest. Whole blocks have been demolished. Owners are leaving houses, both empty and occupied, to rot. A rotting house gets a demolition permit, building land fetches a high price and rents on newly built apartments aren't subject to 'archaic' restrictions. The low rents draw the Turks because they can't afford more, aren't wanted elsewhere and if they hope to save enough to one day return in dignity to their homeland, it might at least be possible here. 'Kebab-

Träume in der Mauerstadt', kebab-dreams in the Wall-city, another *Fehlfarben* line. On some streets every second house is squatted.

Coasting down a side street, she finds herself approaching a crowd, the sound of live music, the smell of meat barbecuing over charcoal. She dismounts and chains her bike to a lamp-post. It's a street party.

There are stalls on both sides of the street: sellers of home-made cakes, the German-Turkish solidarity group, the local tenants' association, free face-painting for children, handmade jewellery, an info-stall by one of the more together squatted houses. She buys a plastic cup of Riesling from a couple selling wine. On a makeshift stage on the back of a lorry a Turkish folklore troupe in traditional costumes is dancing, the oriental music and the pounding of their boots on the stage timbers echoes down the street.

She sees Dmitri, but he - Gott sei Dank[40] - does not notice her. He's sitting on the pavement, pissed as usual, engaged in a shouting match with a group of Punks.

Further down, a crowd has gathered around something. It's a performance by a street theatre group. The evil trinity of speculator, politician and Bulle are seeing the error of their ways and begging forgiveness from the people, represented by a sweet smiling Punk and a bearded hippy with flowers in his hair, a too-big-to-be-true joint in one hand and a regulation-issue anarchist spherical black bomb in the other.

---

[40] Gott sei Dank - Thank God!

She lingers at a book stall. Most of the books are pirated black and white prints of expensive full-colour volumes, the rest obscure political tracts. One catches her eye: a black bible-like tome sporting the red machine-gun insignia of the RAF. She picks it up, drawn by the paradox. It's a collection of position papers and declarations, press releases, interviews. She flicks through it. The Marxist terminology has a bold certainty about it. It dawns on her how little she really knows about the Rote Armee Fraktion. She'd been in secondary school at the time. The time of the wanted posters in the baker's and the butcher's. The time of the crossing-out of the young faces whenever one of them was caught - or shot dead. The time of the Schleyer kidnapping and Mogadishu and the convenient suicides in Stammheim. But these days the posters are confined to police stations and post offices. It costs eight marks. She forgets about it the minute she pops it into her shoulder bag.

A blast of incomprehensible Punk crashes over the PA. She heads towards the stage, buying another Riesling on the way.

"What brings you to this part of the world?" Tina asks, pouring the aromatic Earl Grey. Justine's visit is unexpected.

"I had to collect some papers from my old employers, the Arbeiterwohlfahrt."

The Arbeiterwohlfahrt is a charity which provides home help for pensioners.

"Sugar?"

"One please!"

"What's the work like?"

"Depends on who you get. Some of them just give you the shopping list and the money and let you get on with it. Others mainly just want someone to talk to. Sad really. Not their being old. It's something else ... an air about them that my grandparents don't have. They live in a village near Orleans. They're cantankerous old fogeys. He's a drinker and calls himself a Bonapartist. She's tells him she votes Communist to wind him up - and probably does."

Tina's paternal grandparents had disappeared in East Prussia in 1945. Her mother's parents were smug, intolerant and churchgoing, as if nothing even slightly odd had ever happened in Germany or as if it had all been something of a bit of a mishap best not mentioned. Her father been about eighteen when the war started and spent it in the navy. She had no idea what her mother had done.

Justine lights a filtered Gitane.

"I had four regulars. One old guy - a Herr Marx - used to insist on showing me this photograph of himself as a young man in some ill-fitting Wehrmacht corporal's uniform. And then he'd tell me about when he was in France - totally oblivious to the possibility that I might have had family who'd been killed by the army he'd been in. He was stationed at a customs post in the Pyrenees and he used to tell me how one day they all got drunk on some Calvados some gendarmes gave them. He used to go on and on about it, as if that bottle of Calvados had been the high point of his life, the essence of his youth. Once he actually muttered something about Russia, where they sent him in the end, but all I ever got out of him was that it was very big and very cold."

"Can I nick one of those?"

Justine hands her the blue Gitanes packet.

"The war always comes up. I thought my being French was the reason for it. Sometimes, at first, they thought I was Polish – what with my name – but when they discovered I was French they would talk.

"There was also a Herr Zimmermann. He insisted I call him Frederick. He used to buy me chocolates and offer me drinks. After about the third visit he started going on about how a man needed a woman - even an old gentleman like his good self, and perhaps if I couldn't be nice to him in that way perhaps I had a friend who would. You French understand these things, he used to say."

"What were the women like?"

"One had lost her husband in Russia, at Stalingrad, and had lived alone since. Her father and one of her brothers had died in the east too. But she didn't seem bitter about it. She was the nicest of them. After the war she'd spent twenty years working at Siemens. Empty Jägermeister bottles all over the place."

"Any others?"

"One other, a Frau 'von' Bollendorf. Her husband had been 'ein Offizier' and been shot by the Russians ... after the war, I think he was captured ... and she was bitter. They'd had land in Poland or what's Poland now until 'the Reds' had stolen it from them."

"Well, that's fucking Deutschland for you," Tina says.

German self-hatred always struck Justine as being particularly vehement and deep-rooted.

"So many things are hidden here," Tina says, "especially things that have to do with the war and the past. Everything is clean on the outside, but you dig a bit ... something ugly always turns up."

9

"Ah, the familiar sweet sickly smell ...," Our Hero says, about to inhale deeply.

"Saw a massive one the other day," Horse says, sipping from his glass of cheap Aldi red. "Up by the Wall. It was spread over the two gable-ends of some big buildings. It was two paintings really, I suppose."

Our Hero exhales.

"Of?"

"The spirit of the times, I guess. The first one was of three witches-cum-anarchists around a bubbling cauldron, like in Macbeth, with cartoon-anarchist bombs bubbling out of it, and thunder and lightning, with one of the thunderbolts in a circle making a gigantic Besetzer symbol. The bombs were turning into bubbles and floating up into the air, floating above this ugly-looking norm family sitting in a pile of rubbish - broken television sets, dishwashers, consumer detritus. One of the bubbles had '68 written on it and it had burst. There was also one with '81. Even cynical me was impressed!"

"That's the KuKuCK. K-U-K-U-C-K. Kreuzberger Kunst und Kultur Zentrum."

"Besetzt?"[41]

"Yeah! And recently raided by 400 Bullen."

Horse pours some more Aldi red.

---

[41] Squatted, more literally 'occupied'.

"How's life with Dread these days?"
"Claustrophobic!"
"All we have to do is knock down the walls. Here, I think there's a bit left in this."
Our Hero passes him what's left of the joint.
Horse takes a probing toke.
"Nah, it's dead. But I have plenty more."
"It's getting one over on them – but the hassle, the possibly unnecessary hassle?"
"Fuck the hassle," Our Hero does a John Wayne impression, "A man's got to do what a man's got to do!"
"True enough."
"I'm sick of talking, of eternal yapping about alternatives and all that. I want to do something for a fucking change. I'm tired of the yap-yap-yap."
"Do what thou wilt!"
"Shall be the whole of the Law."
"And Love is the Law."
"Love under Will." [42]

Two days later, Our Hero, naked from the waist up, in shorts cut from an ancient pair of Levis and shod in a pair of worn-out gym shoes, takes the first sledgehammer swing at the bricked-up arch in the kitchen. His first blows are timid. But immediately a hole appears and he can see through it, so he lets go, belting bricks right out of the wall and into the apartment beyond amidst tumbling rubble and rising dust.
It takes about five minutes to break through

---

[42] Aleister Crowley.

completely.

He climbs over the rubble and through the dust into the empty apartment on the other side.

He's done it. He's fucking well done it. He does a hip-hop and laughs aloud at the thought of it.

He sits down on the floorboards and rolls a ciggie. He intends to savour the moment, magically draw it into him with the smoke.

He wipes the grime and the dust from his sweat-drenched forehead with the back of his hand. He feels good.

Through the archway the kitchen of his old apartment is visible through the rubble and dust. It seems in a different world, one he's consigned to the past.

The roll-up becomes a butt. He stubs it out and gets up.

The other wall, a partition of wood, straw and plaster, is a messier job and takes twice as long to dismantle. He sprinkles it with water several times to keep the dust down.

Just as he is about to finish he hears footsteps outside and stops, suddenly conscious of the racket he's been making.

Schreiner's curious face peeps around the door.

"You look like the madman in that *Themroc* film!"

He's carrying a six-pack.

"Direct action to create additional living space. A beer would go down nicely."

Schreiner obliges.

"I'm surprised the old geezer above hasn't been down to complain," Schreiner says, referring to Herr Marx. "You could feel the vibrations up on the third floor."

"He went out earlier. He's okay. I can handle him.

It's the old woman on the fourth floor you have to look out for. She's completely off her head!"

"She waylaid me on the stairs the other day and said she'd heard that there were Besetzer in the house, and had I seen any?"

There's a knock on the door. Polite but firm. They both froze.

"Who is it?" Our Hero shouts.

A hesitant female voice answers.

"My name is Justine."

"Come in," Our Hero shouts, adding unnecessarily that the door is open. "We're in here. To your right."

She clambers over the rubble looking as if she doesn't know what she's walking into, which is exactly how she feels.

Our Hero is sure he's seen her before somewhere.

"Tina said she spoke to you."

"Ah, you're the French woman who might be interested in one of the apartments."

She nods, her dark round eyes beaming.

"Have we met somewhere?" Our Hero asks.

"I used to visit the pensioner upstairs last winter. I was working for the Arbeiterwohlfahrt."

Our Hero explains the situation. Schreiner listens in silence, following them around as Our Hero gives her a guided tour. Eventually they come to the one remaining free apartment. The door is open.

"There was no key, so we had to break the lock."

They go in.

"Scheißßßße!" Schreiner breaks his silence.

The place stinks, as well as being full of junk: rotten armchairs and sofa, two mouldy mattresses, fungus on the wall under the windows, and where the oven should be there's only a hole in the wall to the chimney.

"It looks worse than it really is," Our Hero says. "If the others are agreed, you can have it - if you want it. We'll help you fix it up."

Justine gives him a quick grimace of a smile.

Our Hero spends the first night in the eerily empty apartments alone, waking up shortly after dawn to the sound of police sirens. He doesn't get back to sleep again. Paranoia. Paranoia.

GeWoBag, the owners, turn up the next day. Herr Marx, when he saw Our Hero and Schreiner bringing the rubble out in an old tin bathtub, had gone straight to the office down the street and told them that their tenant, the Herr Irishman, was knocking their house down. A foreman and a clerk had come to see what is happening and inspect the alterations. When they asked him who did he think he was, Our Hero tells them the apartments are now 'officially' besetzt and if they didn't like that, it was their problem - and their fault for leaving the places empty. They leave saying that this is not the last he is going to hear from them. Herr Marx appears later and gives him a present of a bottle of Aldi champagne – saying he hopes there are no bad feelings.

The next few days are confusion, chaos, anarchy, things being done and undone. There's more rubble to be moved, walls plastered, broken window panes replaced, walls whitewashed, floors painted and electricity connected up. Beer, grass, coffee, tea and tobacco are consumed in unhealthy quantities. They even manage to transplant Horse's grass plants to the neglected excuse for a garden out the back.

Tina paints her room in a day, the walls white, the floorboards in a yellow-black chess board pattern. The following day, with the help of Schreiner, over a bottle of Intershop Gordon's Dry Gin and a carton of Aldi orange juice - of which Schreiner drinks more than the lion's share - they put in a high bed made from reused wood.

Horse begins sleeping there a few days later, on the couch in Our Hero's room at first. Each day brings more people to breakfast with it: Tina, Big Bruno. And the evening meals more again: Schreiner, Kalypso, Justine, others.

One morning at about two, Our Hero and Horse stagger back from *Godot,* shouting, thinking they are singing:

Deutschland, Deutschland alles ist vorbei!
Deutschland, Deutschland, all is forebye![43]

Kalypso is furious at them the next morning and lets them know it. They'd woken Fröschchen up. And the rest of the house, Big Bruno adds.

"I read your stories," Horse says.

The window is open but a smell of fresh paint hangs in the air. Our Hero has just finished painting the round table a gaudy yellow. It's the room's centre piece.

One of Dread's reggae tapes is playing.

"Und?"

"Why SF?"

"Because we live in a science fiction world.

---

[43] alles ist vorbei! - it's all over!

Everything is possible, from Utopia - if the aliens land ..."

"Or there's a world revolution."

"... to 1984 to Armageddon. The last at the pressing of a button. Maybe it's a sort of reaction to NO FUTURE, not the Punk variety, the other one, the real No Futurists: the Ronnies and the Maggies, the CDU and Fine Gael[44] voters, the ones who can't see any future beyond their wallets and their mortgages and have the power to make their fantasies real for the rest of us. Or rather their lack of fantasy. Or any kind of imagination."

"I liked *The Last Battle*."

The Last Battle, set in the icy vacuum beyond Pluto's orbit, is about two computer-controlled spaceships, one American and one Soviet, their crews in suspended animation, heading away from a nuke-charred dead Earth towards the nearest habitable planet some twenty light years distant. Both ships are computer-programmed to destroy each other.

"Doris Lessing's first stuff used to be totally straight. Then SF crept in, as if the things she wanted to write about couldn't be written about straight. You've read *Shikasta*?"

It's a bit of a cult book that year.

"An interesting literary exercise. But the idea that there's some fucking aliens out there keeping some sort of benevolent eye on us is wishful thinking."

"Or our only hope?"

"Redemption shall come from on high. A Second Coming in the form of flying saucers. Send out our

---

[44] Irish political party.

radio messages and pray some fucker is listening."

The tape comes to an end. Horse turns it over.

"Put it down for a second," Our Hero gasps.

They put the couch down on the pavement. It's one of those ones that opens out flat and can be used as a bed. They've just carried it down three flights of narrow stairs.

The street is hot after the cool of the courtyard.

"Don't you already have one of these?" Schreiner says. "One exactly the same?"

"I want to put the two of them together and have a decent-sized bed. My love life requires it."

Schreiner raises his eyes to the gods.

They start off again.

The sound of the royal fucking wedding - of Charles and fucking Di - being broadcast live to the whole fucking planet from Saint Paul's Cathedral, or Westminster Abbey or wherever it is, is creeping eerily out of several windows along the street.

Schreiner: "Scheiße, half of Europe must be watching that fucking thing."

"A simple girl of the people is becoming a princess," Our Hero taunts him. "Like in a fairy tale come true. Your Teutonic heart must be as hard as Krupp steel."

"As tender as leather."

They begin to cross Chamissoplatz.

Children, German and Turkish, are playing in the sand pits. Dmitri is sitting with someone at one of the rough wooden tables, a bottle of Aldi red and two glasses in front of them. He waves.

Tina and Big Bruno are playing table tennis.

They reach number 11. Schreiner pushes the heavy

front door open and they manoeuvre the couch into the courtyard. The white reggae sound of *UB40* blares from the open window of the common room. Horse is sitting on the window sill, smoking a joint.

He hands the joint to Our Hero who takes a quick toke from it. He makes to pass it on but Schreiner shakes his head.

"I smoke not hashish," Schreiner says, changing to English. "I also once take a lot of heroin but for six months now I am clean. I take no drugs."

"Except alcohol," Horse says.

"That is different!"

"It was a fucking laugh. Outside one mansion the loudspeaker van informed us authoritatively that it was the villa of anti-social and evil speculator pig so-and-so who owned such-and-such a house in Kreuzberg. Needless to say, an announcement followed by a barrage of boos and paint bombs, but it stopped abruptly when the woman in the van started informing us that there'd been a bit of a mistake, that it wasn't this house, that it was the one next door. She'd mixed up the house numbers."

Big Bruno is in Tina's room telling her about Sunday afternoon's stroll by Besetzer around plush wooded haute bourgeois Grunewald. The *BZ*, splendidly outraged, had carried the story of a 'young' policeman being relieved of his trousers and pistol by the mob on its front page the next day.

"We came across a South African consulate or something which nobody'd known was on the route. Needless to say again, that got the treatment too. In the end the Bullen used tear gas to disperse us, but that only spread us out and made it more difficult for them to control us."

Clouds of tear gas wafting over the idyllic villa suburb of the Grunewald! Kreuzberg has being putting up with it for months. It was good to see the real bastards, not just their lackeys the Bullen, getting a taste of their own medicine.

Interview published in the Magazine:

How did you originally get involved in squatting?

Wilde: Through the Chamisso Tenants' Centre initially. I've lived in this area for years and have been involved in various projects. For example, we catalogued the number of empty apartments in the Kiez[45] as part of a city-wide survey by the Berlin Tenant's Union. We counted at least 10,000 empty apartments in the city. The idea was to get something done for underprivileged groups: migrant worker families, single women with children. The migrant workers were in a situation in which they could do very little for themselves. A lot of them have been living in squalid conditions for years. We had discussions with the Senate but nothing happened - despite the press coverage. We got a lot of verbal concessions and we thought we had made some progress. But we were wrong. Nothing really positive was achieved by it all.

How did the squatting start?

Wilde: Places have been squatted for the last five years. Just before Christmas several houses - in the worst slum clearance area in the east of Kreuzberg -

[45] Neighbourhood.

were evicted. There was a big demonstration on the Ku'damm. The police broke that up quite savagely. That led to the first militant resistance on the streets. At about the same time another building scandal hit the news. The so-called Garski Affair. The Senate ended up losing a hundred million marks of public funds. Heads had to roll, in particular that of the mayor. Hans-Joachim Vogel was sent from Bonn to take his place and prepare for the May elections. This created a kind of power vacuum, a breathing space that various groups and organisations involved in the housing issue used to occupy more empty houses and highlight the general housing situation. The Public Prosecutor's Office and the police wanted to move against them but Vogel needed a quiet city for the elections, and generally the squatters had the support of the Left of the SPD. Before anyone knew what was happening the situation acquired its own momentum. Other groups looking for a free living space - space under their own control - joined in. Soon houses were being occupied at the rate of one a day. The authorities had been caught off guard. The police reacted with searches. The squatters' answer to that was resistance on the streets. The squatting movement, in part, has its roots in the student revolt of '68. The Alternative Liste also has its roots there.

What kind of people are involved?

Wilde: I can only tell you about the people around here, where about nineteen houses are occupied. Students and a fair sprinkling of unemployed and younger people. There are also a few older people who have been active for a long time. And there's also the so-called militant fringe, kids who are to some extent a bit disorientated. My experience with the Punks for instance: they are in some ways very naive, which is disconcerting at times, but behind the facade and the language I have found them to be really nice people. In general, most of those involved are young, intellectual, and politically aware.

How long have you been in this house?

Wilde: Since the beginning of the year. We occupied the three empty apartments in the front house first. Later we opened up apartments in the back house. There are rent-paying tenants living in the house, which can be both an advantage and a disadvantage. They have a different attitude to property. Maybe that keeps our feet on the ground. But it can be difficult to do things in the house. In houses in which there are only squatters the people tend to look on the house as their own and have put a lot of work into changing the interiors and renovating them. They have things like communal workshops. Squatting is not just concerned with housing, it's also about alternative ways of living.

How have the tenants and your neighbours reacted?

Wilde: Fairly mixed. It can be difficult to overcome suspicions. But after a few weeks some tenants were coming by with old carpets and furniture. We organised discussions. At first we didn't have much response. We tried to explain the so-called modernisation plans and how the tenants themselves were affected by them. We put tables on the pavement and invited the people to coffee and cakes and tried to explain why we were squatting. Sometimes it was good and we could really talk with them, but a lot of people still remained cautious, especially because of the association between squatting and violence.

And the Senate?

Wilde: When Vogel took over as mayor he developed a policy involving negotiations with the squatters, but from the start we were not prepared to negotiate while people who had supported us on the streets were still in jail. That is still the case. Nevertheless, discussions have taken place through third parties. From very early on the Senate has being trying to divide the movement, into houses which would negotiate and houses which would not. Looking back on it now, it seems that this was a deliberate tactic to split the movement. During all this searches and evictions continued, very often on the initiative of the police, who wanted to show that they had the upper hand.

The police have searched a lot of houses?

Wilde: Yes. They come very early in the morning and people are hardly ever prepared for them. They've wrecked some of the places they've been into. The squatters have to produce their identity cards and are photographed. Sometimes they are taken to one of the larger police stations to be questioned and have their fingerprints taken. In most cases they are charged with criminal trespass, sometimes with resisting arrest, and with stealing gas and electricity, and even water. In some cases too they've been charged under Paragraph 129a, the conspiracy section of the Anti-Terrorist Laws introduced to combat the RAF.

And support from the general public for the squatters?

Wilde: There is a basic sympathy but it is hard to define. Lots of people, especially in an area like this, at some time or another have had trouble with landlords, with the rents going up, with the neglect of the houses, and especially with the problem of actually getting an apartment. But because of the press coverage, the police provocation, and the form of resistance the squatters have adopted, this sympathy has ebbed. The Springer Press, which controls 80% of the newspapers, has tried to isolate and criminalise the squatters as Chaoten and Radikale. There has been no real discussion in the establishment media of the problems behind the squatting, and no understanding of why people are going out onto the streets and smashing the windows of banks and insurance companies.

Doesn't the violence alienate people?

Wilde: I call it counter-violence. We decided we must always react to the searches and the evictions, to the sort of thing that happened at the beginning of the year when the whole of the Squatters Council was arrested under Paragraph 129a. We can't just let that happen. If we did, they'd be breaking down this door tomorrow and we'd be out on the street. There must always be a political reaction to these attacks. Much of this has been directed into this counter-violence. The original violence is the organised violence of the police and the state. If there were no searches or evictions - and a political solution to the whole problem was being discussed with us - there would be no need for it. People don't go out onto the street and risk prison sentences for fun. They do it to protect what they've achieved over the last six months. As for it alienating people: that is true. But the press will always be against us, no matter what we do.

And the future?

Wilde: If it comes to a mass eviction, there will be a mass reaction. The Senate knows that. The new mayor knows that. In the long run the CDU may try and evict all the houses. And if there's no resistance they will be able to do that.

Anything to add?

Wilde: Yes. The imagination and the work that goes on in the houses. Squatting is not just sitting on your backside and doing nothing. There is fantastic potential in the houses. It would be a pity to see it destroyed by this mindless repression. In many ways the houses are like small plants. In the right conditions they will start to grow and a lot will come out of them. But if you keep tearing them and withholding water, you destroy them. In the houses a lot of people are trying to be creative and sensitive towards their environment, but when there is continuous violence from outside, they become nervous and edgy, and maybe in the long run very resigned. The last few months have shown us that nothing has changed with regard to the Senate's housing policy. Luxury apartments and huge profits are more important than people's needs. There's life in the houses now. Courtyards have been cleaned up and painted. Gardens have been planted.

10

The pool of liquid fire the petrol bomb has splattered across Martin-Luther-Straße is belching black smoke. The massive demo had started peacefully, its destination Rathaus Schöneberg. Twenty minutes later the first teargas canisters were being lobbed into the air over the crowd and the demonstrators had begun to disperse. Horse has never seen a riot before or been in one. It's different from what he had imagined.

Tina runs with the crowd, teargas canisters hissing through the air, landing clattering and bouncing along the street behind them.

"Keine Panik!" people are shouting, "Don't panic!"

The crowd slows down.

The far end of the street is engulfed in a white cloud of pungent-smelling gas that hangs motionless in the still afternoon heat.

They move slowly on, more a group now than a crowd, away from the gas and God knows how many Bullen on the other side of it. There's about fifty of them. Not many. But there are countless groups like them in the streets all around.

She hears the sound of breaking glass.

Somebody is screaming: "Are you crazy?"

She turns around.

Joschka is pelting stone after stone into the glass facade of the building opposite.

"It's a fucking police station," someone shouts.

A guy is prising cobblestones out of the pavement with a screwdriver. Some people start to run. Others help themselves to the cobblestones and throw them at the building, punching jagged holes in the semi-opaque glass panes of the checkerboard facade.

She makes a split-second decision, grabs a stone and flings it. It hits the glass but bounces back. Her second shot doesn't. It cracks the glass of an already cracked window. She grabs another, flings that and moves further up the street.

A mass of olive-green uniforms, too many to be counted, in white helmets and carrying shields, are suddenly visible running down a stairs behind the facade, ducking the stones that are peppering it. She gets one more stone in, but doesn't wait to see where it hits.

"Champagne für das Proletariat!" Dread is shouting, waving a bottle of it about. "Champagne for the proletariat! Champagne for the masses!"

The windows of the Bolle supermarket have been smashed. Crates of beer, schnapps and champagne are being looted. The corks are popping. Sweet German champagne is spurting all over the place.

Dread takes a long deep slug of the sparkling vino.

"Nothing like the smell of tear gas in the morning."

It's great to see people cutting loose like this, absolutely fucking great.

Wilde is breathless. Twice they've made their way up the street that leads onto John-F-Kennedy-Platz and the Rathaus, and twice they've been chased back down it again by baton charges. Several people have been hit, one badly, and someone has been arrested.

This is more or less the front line.

He pulls his scarf down, hoping to be able to breathe more freely, but it's not much use. The tear gas is everywhere. He cough-spits several times in an attempt to clear his lungs. His head is beginning to ache.

On John-F-Kennedy-Platz the Bullen are getting into position in front of the barriers again. They have withdrawn, obviously too overstretched to follow up the baton charges they've made. Which means that they can have another go at the bastards. People are digging up more cobblestones.

Most of those around him seem to know what they are doing. Which is reassuring. Innocent bystanders always seem to end up getting more badly beaten than the activists. Despite the masks and the scarves, he half-recognises some of them - people he knows by sight from around the place.

"We need to build a fucking barricade," one guy is saying. "If they drive down here in their transits we're fucked."

"Those builders' wagons up there should do the job nicely," Wilde says.

The crowd makes its way up towards the Rathaus slowly, digging up more cobblestones on the way, scattering them over the street - for future use.

A woman with a black spray can is graffiting every bit of spare wall she can find:

leben-lieben-lachen! [46]

---

[46] Living, loving, laughing!

legal-illegal-scheißegal!
macht kaputt was euch kaputt macht! [47]

She signs off with a generous sprinkling of anarchist 'A's in circles and Besetzer signs.

People move the builders' wagon into the centre of the street and after a few heaves manage to overturn it. Wilde joins in. It tips over with a smash.

Splash!

A shower of water splatters over the pavement and some parked cars. Wilde looks up.

"Pigs, dirty fucking pigs, they should beat you all to fucking death," an unshaven beer-bellied hulk with a plastic bucket is yelling down at them from a balcony.

Wilde gives him the finger and yells a stream of obscenities back up.

They advance further, overturning another builders' wagon as they do so.

They get to within fifty metres of the Bullen.

An order is barked.

The Bullen form themselves into a phalanx and start to move forward, beating their shields with their batons.

Wilde begins grabbing cobblestones, stuffing them into the pockets of his leather jacket. Everyone does.

Then they rush forward towards the marching Bullen screaming war cries.

They come within of range of the massed shields. The hail of granite bounces off the wall of perspex and stops the Bullen in their tracks. Another volley

---

[47] Make kaput what makes you kaput!

nails them down, but then there's a crack and a teargas canister hisses through the air, heading straight down into them. Seconds later another one follows.

Shit, Wilde says to himself, about to turn and run ... everything now is in adrenalin-induced slow motion ... but this guy in a ski mask and wearing heavy duty industrial gloves has suddenly appeared and is picking up the smoking hot metal canister. He flings it back at the Bullen, then grabs the other one and seemingly effortlessly dispatches that too in the same direction. Both land short of the phalanx, but they stop it advancing. Another hail of cobblestones presses the advantage home.

"Go for their fucking legs!" a tall blond guy, maskless, is screaming. His accent is East European. He is bowling cobblestones along the ground, aiming for the Bullen's unprotected shins beneath their shields.

A Bulle crumples over and is swallowed by the protective shields of his comrades.

"That's the way we do it in Hungary," he says.

Suddenly, to the right of the phalanx there are three flashes, followed by the familiar cracks of the teargas guns firing, but this time not aimed up to land in the middle of them, but on a trajectory that at its highest point is little more than a foot above their heads. The scalding chemical-packed canisters zap right into them. One hits a parked car, bounces off it, missing Wilde by centimetres.

He turns and runs, his eyes on fire. Others are doing the same. It's panic. If someone trips he'll trip over them and someone'll trip over him. He forces his eyes open to scan the ground in front of him, passing the guy with the gloves picking up another one of the canisters and throwing it back. Just when he thought he never would, he emerges from the gas and there in front of him is the overturned builder's wagon. Once behind it someone hands him a plastic lemon and he squirts the acidic juice straight into his eyes. The effect is immediate. He can see again. They haven't been beaten yet.

"There's Justine," Horse says.

Our Hero looks up and sees her come in through the glass doors.

He and Horse have escaped into *Niemandsland* and decided to take refuge in each other's company and alcohol.

She throws her camera onto the table.

"Have you seen Tina?" Our Hero asks.

"About half an hour ago," she says in English, "She was on Winterfeldtplatz with some guy she knows."

"Any good photographs?" Horse asks.

"Maybe."

The crowd on the street outside makes a sudden movement. Our Hero gets up and goes out to investigate.

"Anything happening?" Horse asks him when he comes back in.

Our Hero shakes his head.

"They could pick up a thing or two in West Belfast!" Horse says. "Half of the bods can't seem to make up their mind whether they're rioting or demonstrating."

"And what did you do during the revolution?" Our Hero says, sarcastically quoting a line from a cartoon in the copy of *An Phoblacht* he'd picked up at Dread's.

"Oh, I supported it totally. I was all for it. Can't remember the number of times I spoke out for it in this very pub!"[48]

"I'm going to the bar," Justine says.

While Horse is counting out some money Dread barges in.

"You lot have been missing the crack," he says, barely keeping a damper on his enthusiasm, taking a precautionary look around the place, before giving them a quick glimpse of the bottle of Russian vodka he's hidden inside his donkey jacket.

"Confiscated, comrades. In the name of the people!"

"Bullen are Bullen, East or West," the Hungarian is saying. "When I left Hungary I went to Bavaria. They gave me three months to get out. That's how I ended up here. The two things I hate most are police and borders - and armies. That's how I got into trouble in the first place. I didn't want to do military service and protect the sacred Hungarian fatherland. I believe in socialism, democratic socialism, not the 'real existing' crap they have on the other side of the Wall. Do you want a fag?"[49]

Wilde takes one, a filterless Roth-Händle, strong.

---

[48] *An Phoblacht*, Sinn Fein / IRA newspaper.

[49] Officially the system on the Other Side is not communism, but 'real existierender Sozialismus', real existing socialism. The classless communist society is to come later, and the state will 'wither away' (Vladimir Lenin), or 'die off' (Friedrich Engels). The ruling party in East Germany is the Sozialistische Einheitspartei Deutschlands (SED), officially a coalition of the Communist Party, the Social Democrats and even Christian Democrats and Liberals. Its West Berlin branch is called the Sozialistische Einheitspartei Westberlins (SEW).

The motionless cloud of tear gas still obscures the end of the street. And the Bullen are undoubtedly at the other side of it.

Wilde's eyes are glued to the white haze in case there's any sudden movement. He'd actually been there once. In Hungary ...

Everything happens simultaneously: the engine revving, the flashing blue light, the white and green transit emerging from the gas, screeching to a halt, turning and blocking off the street when the driver suddenly sees the overturned builder's wagon. Wilde and the Hungarian spring into action with the others, launching a hail of cobblestones that bounces off the transit's metal sides and caged windscreen, forcing it to turn and retreat. The stone throwers cheer.

The obvious thing to do now is to set the builder's wagon on fire, and already a red-haired woman in a leather jacket has climbed onto its side, smashed open its flimsy windows and is stuffing burning newspapers into it. Smoke begins to pour out of it and she jumps down. Flames are leaping out of it when more transits emerge out of the gas cloud, their back doors slamming open as they screech to a halt.

The cobblestones begin to fly again. The din of them battering the metal sides and roofs of the transits sounds like a battery of drums being beaten in quick succession.

The first teargas canister, shot from the relative safety of behind a transit's open back doors, descends into their midst. The second and third canisters land behind them. If they don't run now they'll be trapped. Wilde sees the first helmeted shield-bearing figures appear from behind the vehicles as he turns to run and hears another shot from the teargas gun. He moves as fast as his legs will carry him. He gets thirty metres before the whole street is completely engulfed in gas. He begins to choke. He can't see. He trips over something, his legs flinging out of control from under him, and crashes onto the asphalt, sliding several painful feet along the merciless surface under his own momentum .

Suddenly he hears a Bulle's voice screaming down at him.

"Got you now, you fucking bastard!"

The whack of a wooden baton across the side of his neck finishes the sentence. It's followed by another across his shoulders as he instinctively curls up and wraps his hands around his skull.

"They've got someone," he hears someone shout from somewhere.

A cobblestone suddenly hits the ground a few feet from him. Another bounces off the Bulle's shield. More follow. He curls up tighter. The Bulle moves back but now the danger is from the badly aimed sharp-edged lumps of rock landing all around him.

He hold his breath and waits an eternity for it to stop.

At the first lull he's on his feet and heading towards the builders' wagon, the pain in his back and neck spreading to his chest and arms.

Tina and Joschka sit pressed against each other in the packed U-Bahn. The carriage is too full for anything but small talk.

There's something reassuring about him, she thinks. He's comfortable to be with. In Heilbronn he was just one of another crowd. He'd never even been a remote possibility. But, now, after just a few hours wandering the insurgent rubble-strewn streets with him, she isn't just feeling attraction, she's feeling desire.

They change trains at Mehringdamn, go down the escalator and wait on the platform. Neither of them seem able to break the silence between them. She wonders what he's feeling, thinking - if anything.

The train arrives. There's standing room only.

"My legs are killing me," he says, smiling, perhaps a bit too innocently. They are about the same height.

"Mine too. Rioting is serious exercise."

She's thinking they'll be getting off at the next stop and going their separate ways if she doesn't for once take the initiative.

Wilde arrives back at his studio apartment sore and shaking, wanting to be alone, drained yet awake, as if he was coming down from a trip. He sips herb tea and smokes in the dusk, somehow feeling that it would not be right to turn on the light and play a tape and shut out the transit sirens he can hear in the distance and what's probably happening in Kreuzberg 36. His painting of the demo cascading under the Yorckstraße bridges on the easel, nearly finished now, is slowly becoming invisible in the growing summer darkness. Like a portent. But he's not given to such ways of thought. He's gotten a bit of a beating, that's all, hadn't been fast enough, probably getting too old for the game. But, somehow, deep down, he knows it's not as simple as that.

Back in her room, over tea, Tina and Joschka talk for a long time, both surprised at how much they have to say to each other. Neither can quite believe what seems to be happening between them.

Dread begins to run, alcohol and adrenaline pumping through his brain, fleetingly aware of the other people running with him and away from the sudden baton charge. The image of the Sani he'd seen in the doorway trying to help a guy literally soaking in the blood streaming from his skull is fresh in his mind. The shuttered-up shops on both sides of him speed by in the darkness. Like in a film. Wondering where the others are, he looks behind him ... Jesus fucking Christ! A Bulle is almost on top of him. He puts on a burst of speed. Swoosh! A long white hard thing, spinning and slashing, summersaults through the air, misses him by a hair's breadth, lands on the street, bouncing along in front of him to the sound of wood on stone. The bastard's thrown his fucking baton at him. As he passes it he tries to bend down, drop his hand and pick it up, but he's moving too fast. Damn! He runs on, gains distance and reaches people who are not running and knows he's safe.

He leans against some railings, his lungs aching. The air is reeking of tear gas. He's run the full length of Oranienstraße. He's wrecked, and there's still no sign of the others.

They are kissing each other, their lips touching, their tongues exploring, tasting each other. He's almost timid. She had not expected that. It's nice, so nice and so needed. Her softness, her desiring him, the warmth of her awakens in him an intensity and quality of tenderness and desire he had not expected.

They lie together on the deep cushions under her high bed for a while, kissing, caressing, now gently, now with more urgent desire, now simply gazing at each others' reflections in each others' eyes.

"I don't want us to screw," she says after some hesitation "but I want you to spend the night here. I'm not taking anything."

"I understand," he says and gives her a hug.

"Let's go up then," she said, indicating ladder to the bed with an upward movement of her eyes, giving his T-shirt a playful tug.

"Three cognacs and three coffees," Dread orders at the bar.

Our Hero and Justine are at a table. Horse has been nicked. They've rang the Legal Aid Committee but there's fuck all anyone can do until tomorrow and he'll probably be released by then unless they're going to bring him before a judge to get an detention order, which was unlikely.

"You mean he was just standing there, doing nothing," Our Hero is saying.

"He was shouting. He was at the edge of a group of people. They were all shouting, screaming at some Bulle on the other side of the street - and suddenly a pile of them came around the corner out of nowhere and jumped on him."

She's feeling the cumulative effects of the alcohol she's been consuming intermittently all afternoon on a stomach empty save for a donar kebab.

Dread arrives with the goodies.

"If he has any sense he'll play the dumb Ausländer," he says, raising his glass: "Me-no-speaky-Deutschski. Me-lost-tourist. Na zdorovje!"[50]

"Na zdorovje!"

He's drunk too, but not as visibly as Our Hero.

"I think," he says slowly, "that some action is in order. The Commerzbank down by my place is a sitting duck – and the last time I looked it's windows were more or less intact - with all this going on there's no way that there'll be any Bullen up that way."

They put him alone in a cell after they'd processed him, checked his identity and barked at him in broken English. Had he been throwing stones? Why had he come to Germany? Did he have a job? His stomach heaving all through it. But he'd played dumb, and they seemed to have fallen for it, the stupid bastards. He'd also tried the indignant Irish citizen approach, but that had not quite worked. They eventually escorted him down here, pushing him senselessly down the stark corridor. His stomach heaves again. The alcohol, the gas, the stress. He can't hold it down any longer. He makes a rush for the toilet bowl in the floor.

Tina and Joschka sleep a post-orgasmic sleep in each other's arms.

Normally it would have scared her out of her wits, but the day, the alcohol, all that has happened, Horse's arrest, those madmen in uniform tearing down

[50] Ausländer - foreigner, literally 'outlander'.

Oranienstraße belting out mindlessly at anyone and everyone makes Justine past caring about possible consequences as they fling the cobblestones at the Commerzbank windows.

"Smash them all!" Our Hero screams. "Smash them all!"

The sound of cracking glass and then the alarm siren howling reverberates up and down the empty street.

When Dread smashes the last one they turn and run, coming to a stop about a hundred metres on, when it becomes obvious that no one's following. They are breathless.

The Wall is on the other side of the canal, illuminated along the whole of its length to near-daylight by flood lights.

"Know what?" Dread says.

He hates the bastards on the Other Side as much as the ones on this side.

The other two look at him and see the conspiratorial grin.

"I think we should have a go at these fuckers here," he says, nodding in the direction of one of the watchtowers. "At least lob a few stones over. After all, we've had a go at western capitalism and fair's fair."

One look at each other. They're game.

But lobbing stones over the Wall is always a bit of an anticlimax. They just land, ignored like rubbish tossed from a passing train or something – though no doubt registered in some Stasi file as an incident at the Anti-imperialist Protective Wall – on the death-strip among the rabbits and the rolls of barbed wire.

11

Kalypso, Tina and Heidi are in the courtyard, basking in a gradually shrinking rectangle of sunshine. All three are in shorts, barefoot and drinking fresh coffee.

"That could come down for a start," Heidi says, indicating the high crumpling wall that separates the courtyards. "We'd get some more sun."

The courtyard is cluttered. Bikes chained to the rusty railings around the cellar steps. Rubbish bins. Furniture left out to rot like the old armchair Heidi is lounging in. Tina is sitting on an upturned wooden crate the same as the one they're using as a table.

"A few plants wouldn't go amiss either," Tina adds.

"The window frames and house doors could do with a slap of paint," says Kalypso. "And a sandpit for the children."

"And maybe some half-decent tables and chairs," says Tina, "might encourage the pensioners to emerge out of their apartments now and again. The Herr Marx never has any visitors. He only comes down to go to Aldi. And I've only seen the madwoman on the top floor once."

In the silence that follows she gets up and disappears into the house. A few minutes later she returns carrying two half-used tins of paint, some old brushes in a jam jar of white spirit and strips of sandpaper.

"No time like now," she says.

"What colours do you have?" Kalypso asks.

"Yellow and orange."

Tina starts to sandpaper the peeling poison-green door to the back house.

"I rarely make quick decisions," says Justine.

She and Horse are sitting on the wall in Chamissoplatz, waiting to have a go on the table-tennis table.

But there were exceptions, like the way she decided to come to Berlin.

"I know I should make up my mind but ..."

Horse nods. He's made clear often enough his willingness to help her clean out the room. So have the others.

She can't quite decide what it is that's holding her back. The state of the place? Or the insecurity of the whole Besetzer thing?

Their turn at the table-tennis table comes.

As they play her eyes are drawn again and again to a group of Turkish women sitting on a bench behind Horse. Wrapped in scarves and long dresses, they seem old before their time. Some of them are obviously younger than herself. It makes her angry to think of them there, almost veiled, rigid, daring to take up only so much space, smilingly apologetic, while she moves freely, her arms and legs bare to the sun and air.

Horse is creeping ahead, but she concentrates and is soon in the lead again, not that it really matters who wins but she does get a kick out of beating men - not that Horse is the macho type.

On the other hand, she's been over it often enough in her mind and every time she comes to the same

conclusion: move in, take the plunge!
She wins 21-17.
"Another round?" Horse suggests.
She tosses him the ball.
"Your serve."
She wins the first point easily.
"I'll start tomorrow," she shouts at him as he goes to retrieve the ball. "I'll start cleaning out the room tomorrow."

Tina climbs onto the bed and kisses Joschka again.
"I've put the coffee on," she says.
"Come back to bed!"
He's aroused and cosy and wants her.
She shakes her head.
"I'm going to go out and buy some breakfast. We can eat it in here. The common room is in a mess - as usual."
"Where are the IRA?"
"They didn't come back last night. Probably kipped at their so-called office. Our Hero said something about having to get the Magazine to the printers."
She begins to dress.
The windows are open. It looks like it was going to be another scorcher.
"We could go to the lakes," she says.
"I'd like to, but I've got a few things to do."
"Huh! Now who's being serious?"
His seriousness is fighting against the way the world is organised. Hers is more personal.
"When I was at the uni I went around with a digital watch in my head and planned my life out in a peacenik diary," she says.

It's a statement of how much she thinks she's changed.

Gestetnered flyer:

TUWAT will be like Tunix, only the opposite.[51] The West Berlin CDU Senate wants to evict nine squatted houses. How are we going to react to this? How are we going to stop it? Waldemarstraße has had the IDEA that something like Tunix can be organised, only this time it will be TUWAT. With 3,000 squatters in Berlin it must be possible! But where do we start?

We've started by producing this leaflet. We are passing it on to our typesetting, printing and alternative newspaper friends. They will hopefully take over the publicity and propaganda side of things and get the word out - to Hamburg, Frankfurt, Freiburg, Bremen, Munich, Zurich, Basel, Amsterdam, Groningen, London, Liverpool, Copenhagen, Stockholm, Paris, Rome, Naples, Belfast, Milan, Madrid, the Basque country, East Berlin, Moscow, Prague and Warsaw.

We need to inform everyone we know in West Germany and abroad! Send them leaflets and posters! The alternative press must be kept up to date with developments. Leaflets and posters must be printed - and distributed. Info centres need to be set up, be open round the clock and have telephones. All media groups must be activated - video groups, pirate radio stations.

[51] 'tuwat' is a slang expression meaning 'do something', while 'tunix' means 'do nothing'. Tunix was an action organised in 1978 in Berlin by the so-called Spontis.

Food: Kneipen, cafés must organise regular meals for those who come. Field kitchens will be needed.

Accommodation: every squatted house, and that means EVERY squatted house, needs to arrange sleeping places and inform the TUWAT info centres so that they can co-ordinate the allocation of places.

We need to form action groups to plan street parties, meetings, exhibitions, films, music, theatre and other happenings. These action groups will need to work together. Representatives of each one can meet to organise bigger things: demos, events at the Technical Uni, in the Hasenheide. Prison groups can hold events on prisons. The same goes for groups involved in other things, such as police repression, NATO, Ireland, Latin America, nuclear power, housing, unemployment, urban guerrillas, music and street theatre.

Netzwerk and other organisations must be asked to give money. That will also have to be organised.

We'll build defensive villages on all the squares of Berlin and fill the city with Chaoten, terrorists, Punks, hippies, tramps, alcoholics, gays, lesbians, Kraakern[52], rastas and crazies. This city must bubble and boil and stink. The autumn must be long and hot.

We need to mobilise at all levels - the AL, unis, schools, local areas, VIPs.

A lot of people are on holiday but if we really get stuck in, surely we can get it on its feet within three weeks.

We have no choice. We either resist or give up.

---

[52] Kraakern - Dutch squatters.

The establishment already has the shits. Chief Pig Lummer[53] is already squealing for Federal Police and the Civilian Police Reserve.

Can we hope for 50,000 people? Why not? We can try!

Publicise this leaflet in our papers, our radios and all our other media outlets, but especially through word of mouth, the most effective media outlet of them all.

Stick it up in every toilet!

Publicise TUWAT with articles and graffiti!

Organise!

Don't hide your ideas in your heads! Live them!

Send this to your friends! Photocopy it!

Above all COME! For ONE DAY or ONE MONTH, but COME!

Turn the Autobahns into bicycle lanes!

Turn BÄRLIN into the biggest kindergarten ever!

The bricks and bottles of Brixton were Charles and Di's wedding present!

Prove that we are wrong, that we underestimate ourselves!

Come to TUWAT in Berlin and tear down all the walls!

Let's blow ourselves up - out of our own isolation!

Contact address: Mieterrat Waldemarstraße 29, 1000 Berlin 36. Tel 65 12 52.

The long-haired moustached guy wraps up a bundle of 'Tuwat für Tuwat' leaflets in a copy of the

[53] Heinrich Lummer, Innensenator, in charge of the Berlin police.

Tagesspiegel, sticks his head out the door to check that Willibald-Alexis-Straße is free of Bullen and leaves *Café Krautscho*.

"Shall we start?" Rudi says, raising his voice above the din.

There are about ten people in the place, most of them engaged in criss-cross conversations punctuated by the sound of coins dropping into the plastic cup on the pamphlet-strewn desk to pay for the coffee and the bottles of Schultheiß.

"The basic idea of this first meeting," he says, "is to discuss generally what we can do locally - and try and work out a rota so we can have this place open every day for the next seven weeks."

Somebody suggests they do the rota first.

Heike, from the same house as Rudi, sketches a rough table on a sheet of A4 and passes it around to be filled out.

"We also need to organise work groups," Rudi continues.

Tina signs up for Wednesdays. Joschka has himself put down for Thursdays.

"At the moment the most important thing is the publicity," Rudi goes on.

"Propaganda," Dmitri shouts from the corner.

"... but the people in Waldemarstraße are handling that end of things fairly well. All we have to do here is distribute the stuff. But they do need the 'Tuwat für Tuwat' leaflet translated. They've had some translations done but it appears that most of them are pretty crappy."

Our Hero volunteers to do one into English. A woman with a ring in her nose says she knows a Dutch woman who might help, her Austrian accent melodic in comparison to mixture of Szene-Deutsch and Berlinerisch nearly everyone else is speaking. Her name is Ursula.

"What about T-shirts?" Dmitri says.

He's sober today, articulate. But he's helping himself to more of the crate of Schultheiß than anyone else.

"Those white T-shirts cost almost nothing and there's a place in Mehringhof that will print slogans on them dirt cheap. We could have Tuwat printed on them. They can't arrest people just for wearing a T-shirt. Can they? And if they did, it'd be great propaganda."

The suggestion might be taken more seriously if it was from someone else.

"They'd look stupid," Joschka says. "We'd look like something from fucking Disneyland. That's the kind of mass uniformity we want to get away from, isn't it? We'd be like people who go around with Coca Cola and Marlboro ads plastered all over them."

Dmitri raises his eyes to heaven, shakes his head and says he's going to go ahead with the idea anyway - on his own. Not that anyone believes he will.

"I don't think we're going to have many problems with publicity." It's the familiar boom of Big Bruno's voice. He's just come in. "Not with the way the *BZ* and Napoleon Bonaparte Lummer, not to mention the TV, are foaming at the mouth. Banning the leaflets is the best publicity they could have given us. It'd be better still if they banned the whole thingamajig. That'd get 'em coming here in droves. The more the pigs overreact and fall for our propaganda, the better."

"Does anyone know exactly what actions our benevolent masters have actually taken?" Ursula asks.

"I was in the Waldemarstraße this morning," Joschka informs her. "The Bullen had already been. They'd confiscated some leaflets, maybe a few hundred. But the things are being printed on every available alternative printing press in the city."

"They've searched cars that look as though they belong to Freaks going to Wessiland at Dreilinden. and confiscated any they found," Rudi adds, "but they're being printed in Wessiland as well."[54]

"I think it's really important that we use our personal contacts," Ursula says. "If we all wrote ten letters and asked the people we wrote to contact their friends, word would really get out. There are at least 3,000 Besetzer in Berlin."

There's murmured agreement.

"It's got to work on an individual basis as well," Heike adds. "Or it won't work at all."

Rudi feels they're beginning to go off in tangents.

"The publicity is being managed. The most important thing for us here, it seems to me, is what exactly are we going to do here in this Kiez."

"We could organise a street party for the first day?" Muck says. The idea has just come to him.

"Without applying for permission," someone adds amidst the general murmurs of approval.

"The Chamissoplatz street party is on that day anyway," Big Bruno says.

Rudi makes a note in block letters on his pad.

---

[54] West Berlin is completely surrounded by the Deutsche Demokratische Republik (DDR), East Germany, the Other Side. There are several official entry points to the city for those travelling by road from West Germany and through the DDR: Dreilinden and Staaken (mentioned later) are two of them.

"Any other ideas? The sooner we can say that we're doing something, the easier it'll be to get the details onto the general Tuwat programme that the Waldemarstraße people are going to get printed."

"Would this time next week be okay?" Big Bruno asks.

"I suppose so."

"Then we all have a week to think about it," Big Bruno says. "And if people just drop the details into here during the week, we can have a proper list by then."

"Whoever's here," a guy at the door adds, "should make a list of available sleeping places. And maybe we should put notices up around the place - in the *Chamisso Galerie* and the Tenants' Centre - asking people who have places to come here and put their names down."

Dmitri helps himself to another beer, casually pretending to forget to drop a mark in the plastic cup. Rudi gives him a half-hearted dirty look.

"Mañana," Dmitri mumbles and proceeds to immerse himself into listening to the discussion which is rapidly degenerating, or evolving - depending on your point of view - into a free-for-all.[55]

Muck starts to roll a joint.

---

[55] Mañana - Spanish for 'tomorrow'.

12

"Christ, what are you doing?" Horse asks. "This place stinks.

"Trying to disguise this thing," Our Hero says, referring to a leather jacket he has draped over the back of a chair.

He gives the spray can another shake.

Horse had nicked the jacket in a Ku'damm disco a few nights previously. The next morning, feeling bad about giving in to his kleptomaniac tendencies yet again, he'd made a present of it to Our Hero. They'd burned the identity card they'd found in it.

"Is it unrecognisable now?"

Horse shakes his head, though paranoia is one thing he does understand.

"How did the Tuwat meeting go?"

"Quite good. I said I'd translate the Tuwat leaflet into English. Give me a hand if you like."

"Sure. As long as we obey the first principle of propaganda writing ..."

"And what's that?"

"There's only one thing worse than believing the enemy's propaganda ..."

"And that is?"

"Believing your own propaganda."

"This stuff dries fairly quickly, doesn't it?" Our Hero says, referring to the spray paint he's put on the leather jacket.

"Think so."

Horse sits down on the bed.

"The meeting was good," Our Hero says. "People were really enthusiastic."

"The spirit was among them."

"Something like that. They're already talking about calling up the police reserve - the last time they did that was in '68 - and even bringing in Bullen from West Germany - which strictly speaking, is illegal under the Four Power Agreement."[56]

Our Hero puts a finishing hiss of silver on the sleeves of the jacket.

"According to which anarcho-lawyer?"

In Ireland politics is about people killing each other, or starving themselves to death right now as they speak.

"I'd like to put a slogan on the back of this," Our Hero says.

"What about BIG BROTHER IS BEING WATCHED?"

Typewritten notes taken by Our Hero for an article in the Magazine:

> winterfeldtstr 211, 213: 2 houses joined together. lots of space. squatters seem more intellectual/studenty than the average. jürgen showed us around. they've done a lot of work. planning to have a 'father of the constitution' - one of the people who drew it up and is sympathetic to the cause - stay with them as a sponsor. would allow either me or horse

[56] The Four Power Agreement - agreement between the USA, the USSR, Great Britain and France on the post-war legal status of Berlin.

to stay in the house to report on the eviction. a good balcony to take photos from if we decide to. not at all a 'heavy' crowd. can expect passive resistance.
luckauer-str 3: in kreuzberg. down a back street right up against the wall. lots of flags and banners draped out the windows. Front house-door shut. disgusting smell. notice on door said the stink, caused by buttersäure[57], was put there by lummer, springer and co. a young woman opened the door. said she was alone except for another woman who was sick, but if we came around tomorrow at seven we could have a look around. they are having a public meeting tomorrow too at 8 - maybe we'd be interested in attending it? a general air of paranoia and state of siege about the place. horse nicknamed the place 'apocalypse now'.
dieffenbachstr 8: impressive in many ways. the people were outside at a table with a petition against the evictions. asked us to sign. told them who we were and what we wanted. two very young punky girls showed us around. one of them had a pet rat. very friendly and glad to see us. they've done a lot of work and are doing more, despite the threat of eviction. showed us the courtyard. they were painting it and intend turning it into an open-air café. on saturday they plan to have breakfast outside on the pavement and later readings in the house by 'famous' poets and writers. one of them they insisted was 'very famous' - a maximilian somebody or other. both of them were berliners. they had also done

[57] Butyric acid, a component of vomit, a stink bomb.

up the rest of the house. however, it had been in fairly good condition when they moved in. some of the apartments are still occupied by tenants - a turkish and a yugoslav family. said they had a good relationship with them both. promised to send them some copies of the zine.

More from Our Hero's typewritten notes:

public meeting in luckauer-str 3: arrived too late to be shown around house. on original hit list but they have just received an invitation to talks from the owners. they are suspicious. don't trust them. also don't want to betray or compromise the movement by unilateral action.
one woman - annette - did most of the talking. got the impression that most of them did not have much confidence in the effectiveness of meetings.
given lots of details about plans for the house, planning permission applications etc. the usual story.
audience sometimes looked as if they were there to fill out an evening.
most of them were the type of young middle-class german intellectual, politically orientated and aware, but who would never squat a house themselves for fear of the consequences it would have on their careers. berufsverbot? (but isn't that is only for hardcore card-carrying commies?)[58]

---

[58] Berufsverbot - Communist or communists (with a small c) can be excluded from certain jobs in the public sector, e.g. to work as teachers.

history: this is the third group to occupy the place. the other two groups left because of police harassment. the first meets of the squatters council took place here. in fact, it was founded here. the famous mass arrest under the paragraph 219 anti-terrorist thing also took place here. there's been several searches since - and a lot of 'coverage' from the springer rags.
asked why they didn't pay for the electricity. horse's idea - provocative bastard! said they're being criminalised anyway with the searches and various arrests, paying it would make no difference to that.
would they accept a five-year licence to stay? no. why should they? they want a general solution to the problem, and why should they pay rent to firms who exploit their tenants, especially the pensioners and the ausländer. wanted to stress that they were interested in alternative ways of living and in trying to make the area liveable in - an area which for all its shit they find to be a more human environment than the new housing estates. there's life on kreuzberg's streets. bit of a public relations job. contact: annette.
idea for another article: paddies in berlin. came to me as we were going into the besetzer-eck for a beer and saw 'ira/inla' written on the road in metre-high letters. besides visiting paddy pubs and asking people what they think of the hunger strikes and h-blocks and all that, could also visit the bobby sands pub in the besetzt house on bülowstr. actually, that is on

```
the hit list too, so we should visit
it. paddy angle might be good for
ads.
```
[59]

Horse and Kalypso squirt tubes of blue, yellow and red paint onto the virgin-white walls of Horse's room.

When they've finished the thick multicoloured paint freckles the walls with blobs of various shapes and sizes, most of them with tails like comets.

Horse looks at it and makes a face.

"Not exactly what I expected."

Justine has also started painting her room.

Mondbogen gets up from the floor, bows slowly to the sunlight streaming through the window and begins to dress. She's at ease now, in tune with her body and the earth, the way she usually feels after her morning yoga session.

She sits down again, cross-legged, and eats her bowl of grated apple, muesli and fruit juice. Her private peace mission had begun in Washington. Checkpoint Charlie is the nearest she has managed to get to Moscow, that other pivot of the axis of pathetic old men who ruled through fear.

There's a demonstration today, one to do with this thing Tuwat. She plans to get some flowers and distribute them to the demonstrators, and to the police.

---

[59] The H Blocks refers to Long Kesh Prison / the Maze Prison in Northern Ireland where IRA and Loyalist prisoners are imprisoned. IRA prisoners are on hunger strike demanding to be recognised as political prisoners / prisoners of war. Bobby Sands is the first hunger striker to die, on the 5 May 1981. He had been elected to the UK Parliament earlier in the year.

She thinks of the words of that poem again:

Long after
The mythical Aquarian Age of peace
Has dawned on a dead world;

Is it really going to be like that, she wonders. A cataclysm and then a starting all over again?

At the dawn
A naked woman
Her breasts firm with milk
And a naked child
Will walk along a seashore.

Yet, for all its dreadfulness, it's a reassuring vision, one of the cosmos and the earth renewing itself no matter what humanity does. She has no doubt that everything is moving towards the time of crisis, of wēijī, the time of danger and opportunity. She wonders what the author is like for a moment, but then puts her mind to where she is going to get some cheap, or better still, free flowers.

Justine starts putting the last of the rubbish into a black bin bag. The back kitchen, which she'd eventually decided to turn into a darkroom, is slowly getting there. She'd chiselled the damp crumbling plaster away and taken up the rotten floorboards but the musty fungus smell still lingers. Tomorrow she'll start plastering the walls.

She's covered in dust and sweat, but she feels clean, alive and purified, like after good sex, your body smeared with sweat and dried sperm and …

She finishes up and decides to make coffee. She's glad she's decided to move in. It's brought her out of herself in some way. Maybe it's the amount of people who're always around the place. Or just the fact that she's moving into somewhere kind of permanent. Big Bruno and Our Hero assure her that the place will be one of the last to be evicted. Though this summer the future seems to be an extremely nebulous entity. Maybe it's just as well to have a healthy disregard for the future - or the No Future - to plough on regardless, despite the horrors and the shit, the Bomb, rapes and war, the Third World - and what the politicians, who have the nerve to call the Punks 'nihilists', are turning the world into.

She switches on the boiler and looks for the coffee things.

Except for Our Hero behind his closed bedroom door making a sporadic racket at his typewriter, the place is empty. And the common room is in a fucking mess.

Glancing through the window to the sun-lit courtyard she sees that the two Turkish girls have come in to play again. They're drawing hopscotch squares on the concrete ground with lumps of masonry. They're a pest usually, climbing in through the windows the second your back is turned, nicking things and as cheeky as hell. In fact, it's uncannily still, only the sound of Our Hero's typewriter and, somewhere in the distance, the receding chop-chop-chop of one of the helicopters that regularly patrol the perimeter of USAF Tempelhof.

She knocks at Our Hero's door.

"How's your paranoia today?" she jokes.

He makes a face.

The day or rather the night before yesterday he and Dread - in another fit of drunken rebelliousness - had decorated the walls of the local Aldi. On the way back from the demo they'd seen one of the special anti-graffiti Bullen units painting over some previous work. They'd come back to the apartment, finished a bottle of Intershop something or other, come up with the brilliant idea of undoing the damage – as it were – and gotten a few pots of paint together. They'd written Tuwat, IRA/INLA and drawn a few crude shamrocks on the wall, and then for good measure written 1-2-3-let-the-prisoners-free, the Besetzer rallying cry, across the street. Dread had relished describing the whole escapade over early afternoon breakfast the following day. He'd told Our Hero that he'd actually signed his name to it. Our Hero had actually gone down to make sure he hadn't.

"When is the next issue of the Magazine coming out?" she asks.

"We're no longer involved in it."

"Why not?"

"The usual collective rows. Personality clashes. Political clashes. The whole thing was too much on the democratic centralist side for our liking. Hippy tendency." [60]

There's a photo of a riot cop in the *taz*, visor up, his eyes blacked out so as not to be identifiable, a rose stuck in his belt. The caption reads: The rose distributor recommended he 'take it easy'.

---

[60] Democratic centralism - principle of internal organisation of Eastern European Communist parties; decisions made by higher bodies are absolutely binding on lower bodies and party members, and no internal opposition is allowed.

Big Bruno nods in the direction of the Passionskirche stall: "Even Jesus is supporting us."
"Oh, give them a break," Kalypso says, "they're sponsoring some of the houses."
They make their way across Chamissoplatz. The square is packed. Music is blaring from the stage. The air is thick with the sweet smoke of barbequing. The smell of roasting meat hangs in the summer air. There's stalls galore: wine, the SPD, kebabs, beer, books, solidarity committees, games and puppets. A pile of kids and toddlers are queuing up to get their faces painted. And lots of familiar local faces: Dmitri with his eternal bottle of Schultheiß in a crazy Tuwat T-shirt, Heidi with some people from the *Chamisso Galerie*. Our Hero chatting away in English to some Chinese-looking woman in shorts. It's like this every year and like any other street party really, except this one is theirs.

Tina is in *Café Krautscho* with Ursula while the street party is going on. It's been quiet all afternoon, only two or three people have dropped in. A transit pulls up outside.
For a second they think it's only going to park there, to keep a eye on the festivities, but the Bullen start getting out and the Oberbulle walks in the door, followed by the others.
"Search," he announces.
The place is squatted so they don't need a warrant.
"Identity cards, bitte," says another.
Another one starts rummaging through the piles of leaflets on the desk while another goes through the drawers.

Ursula doesn't have her identity card with her.

"Why not?" he asked in that offhand friendly Bulle manner. He's young, sports a blond moustache, and is tanned - obviously just back from his summer holidays.

"I never have it on me. As a matter of principle!"

The Oberbulle is examining Tina's.

"Nice photograph. But a bit of a transformation since it was taken. Not Papa's and Mama's little girl anymore, eh? Not from the way you look now anyway."

"Drugs and bad company probably," remarks the tanned one, in a mock serious tone, smiling at her.

"Very funny."

One of the others begins to take away bundles of the leaflets.

"Read them as you're at it," Ursula shouts after him. "If you can."

Then she says to Tina, loud so the Bullen will overhear: "I sure am glad we don't live on the Other Side. They actually censor things there!"

"There's no comparison," says the Oberbulle, "and you know that as well as I do. They'll be handed over to the Public Prosecutor and if they are not found to be inciting people to break the law, you'll get them back. I'm sorry, but we'll have to take you along with us too, just to check out your identities. You'll be free in an hour if you co-operate."

"We have to make sure that you are not wanted terrorists, you know," the tanned one wisecracks, obviously enjoying it all, as they are led out the door.

13

The sequence of events that follow are not unforeseeable. It's announced over the PA that the Tuwat office has been raided and two women have been arrested. A small crowd makes its way up Freisenstraße to the police station to demand their release. They are dispersed by a baton charge - a pretty half-hearted one - and before anyone knows what's happening a building site is being dismantled and a barricade erected across Willibald-Alexis-Straße, cutting the Bullen off from Chamissoplatz – symbolically at least. By then Tina and Ursula have been released, they have been let out the back door of the police station.

"Come on, give us a hand," Joschka is shouting at no one in particular, trying to pull the wooden fence around the building site down. Two guys, both wearing masks, begin to help him.

Our Hero and Horse exchange looks.

"It looks like the peasants are revolting," Horse smirks.

Without further ado, and with an air almost of inevitability, Horse starts carting bricks over to put on the barricade. Our Hero joins him. About twenty people are doing the same.

Big Bruno is standing with Heidi in the doorway of Wilibald-Alexis-Straße 11. She has a key and is ready to let people into the courtyard and lock the house doors if the Bullen suddenly advance from their positions down the street to try and take the barricade.

"Here we go again," Big Bruno half-laughs, shaking his head.

The music from Chamissoplatz has stopped. The stalls are being quickly dismantled. A lot of the people have already gone, but the crowd milling around the barricade is growing. The light is fading.

Heidi overhears some people who obviously don't know each other arguing.

"This is just shitting on your own doorstep. Why don't they go and do it on the Ku'damn, and hit the capitalist state where it really feels it - in its pocket!"

"You just can't let them get away with this sort of provocation. They've just smashed their way into that Besetzer café and arrested two people who weren't doing anything - and right in the middle of a street party. That's deliberate provocation."

"The Bullen think they own the place. Whose street is it anyway?"

"Building a barricade is only asking for it. There are still people with kids down on Chamissoplatz!"

"The barricade is there to protect the people on Chamissoplatz."

"Bullshit!"

He's right of course, Heidi thinks. The young Punk girl's idea of it being a protection rather than an unconsidered act of anger is naive to say the least.

One of the guys in masks starts setting the barricade alight.

It burns slowly. People gather around the flames as

they would around a bonfire. They sit in its glare on the edges of the pavement and on windowsills, talking, drinking, smoking. Cobblestones are being dug up.

Darkness comes and the gas lights go on, but people climb up the lamp posts and put them out. Except for the light from the burning barricade the street is immersed in darkness. The two Kneipen on Chamissoplatz, *Schlemihl* and the *Krug,* are doing a roaring trade. It's a kind of stalemate. Momentary panic breaks out now and again when someone thinks they see some movement down by the police lines. The fire brigade tries to get through - but it withdraws after someone throws a cobblestone in its general direction.

The fire goes out, and all that's left is glowing embers and blackened bricks strewn across the cobbled street. People gradually begin to realise that the next time the Bullen make a move it'll be for real.

"They'll be coming any minute now," Joschka is shouting.

It's impossible to make out how many Bullen there are. Hopefully the Bullen can't tell how many they are either - though by now they've had ample time to slip a few Zivis into the crowd. The guy who set the barricade alight - Joschka recognises him from the graffiti on his leather jacket - is throwing the remnants of some planks onto it. But there's fuck all left to burn at this stage. The familiar clickitty-clackitty-click of seasoned and would-be street fighters banging cobblestones together is starting up.

Our Hero can just make out the silhouettes of Tina and Heidi in the doorway of Willibald-Alexis-Straße 11. There's no sign of Horse.

"Stone throwers up front," a woman shouts, her voice muffled by the yellow scarf covering her face.

Our Hero follows her cue but whether he'll actually have the nerve to do it is another question. He's never thrown stones at human beings before – well not since he was about twelve. The argument that they are wearing full protective armour and he's only in T-shirt, shorts and gym shoes doesn't quite square, ethically. And Christ, he's not even masked.

But he finds some reassurance in seeing familiar faces: Joschka, Schreiner and Big Bruno, and a woman he'd seen at the Tuwat meeting.

"Scary, isn't it?"

It's Horse.

It is. As the man said, bravery is basically a lack of imagination.

All they can make out in the darkness at the end of the street is the odd reflected glimmer on a shield or helmet.

"Seems a bit naff to me," Horse is saying, "standing around exposed like this. They could easily come up on us from behind. The square is deserted except for the crowd outside the *Krug*.

"If they did, we wouldn't have any way out and they always leave an exit. Their main aim is to disperse crowds, not hem them in."

The statement sounded lame.

Suddenly the Bullen start to advance, or seem to, and a half-hearted volley of cobblestones is unleashed.

"Don't panic! Don't panic!" the woman with the

yellow scarf shouts.

Other voices take up the familiar cry.

Nobody seems to know whether it's a false alarm or the real thing. People who had turned to run stop and come back.

But then there's a crack and a flash and then a teargas canister, hissing and belching a tail of white smoke, is bearing in on them.

Time slows down.

It's now or never. Our Hero flings his first stone. In his heart, realising the sheer force he has thrown it with and the momentum it would gather, hopes that it will only hit a shield - if anything. Then he runs for it, past people who are blindly flinging more stones. The cloud of white gas is filling the street. He sprints with the crowd into the empty darkness of Chamissoplatz. He means to throw the second stone, but there's too many people between him and the Bullen who are now emerging charging from the gas cloud. He lets it drop and runs down the cobbled street, passing the crowd outside the *Krug* who are making a desperate rush to get inside, and makes his way into the perceived safety of one of the side streets.

"That's the CDU for you," the guy from the *Chamisso Galerie* is saying to his mate at the bar in the *Krug* about an hour later. "Expect more of it."

"Bullshit!" A young woman standing beside them butts in. "The Bullen were exactly the same under the SPD. There's fuck all difference between them."

"The Tweedledum and Tweedledee theory of politics," he says. "Give me a break."

Schreiner, huddling over a potent Urbock beer, sees

Justine come in.

"What's been happening?" she asks. She's been at the lakes and has just come back.

He tells her, more or less, finishes his Urbock and goes to the bar for another bottle.

Joschka and Tina appear.

"A pre-Tuwat action on the part of the Bullen," Joschka says. "Something to remind us who's in charge."

"Part of the great conspiracy, I suppose," Tina says.

"You saw that Verfassungsschutz letter," he says. Copies of it had been distributed during the week.[61]

"Any idiot with a typewriter could have done that," she says.

His innocence and naivety went hand in hand.

"It could also be genuine," he counters rather half-heartedly. "And there was that article in *Zitty* - speculative of course - which suggested that the Bullen might use the Chamissoplatz street party as a pretext to get tough before Tuwat."[62]

Horse is in the kitchen pouring a two-litre bottle of the real cheap Aldi red - a mixture from six East European countries - into himself when Our Hero comes back. He looks in a state.

"Christ, I need a drink!"

Our Hero helps himself to a glass.

"Just been down in the *Krug*. The place was fucking packed with pub revolutionaries stuffing themselves sick with drink. The gallery crowd and the Tenants

---

[61] Verfassungsschutz - the intelligence service, literally 'Protectors of the Constitution'.

[62] Zitty - one of Berlin's events magazines.

Centre crowd waffling on about tactics. One guy was even going on about how it was in '68. Enough to make you puke!"

He finishes the glass in one go and fills it up again.

"Schreiner was well out of it. He told this SPD guy that the SPD were as bad as the Nazis and the SPD guy was screaming at him that anyone who said that was either evil or stupid or both. Then Schreiner says, cool as a breeze, after they'd been roaring at each other for about ten minutes: 'Or they might just be taking the piss!' - and started laughing his head off. You look positively in pain – as Schopenhauer might say?"

"Just a wallop from a Bulle's baseball bat across the back of my shoulder, that's all. It hurts, but it's more the shock than anything. The cunt just missed my head by inches."

Later, after Our Hero has gone upstairs to Heidi, borrowed some herbal ointment and is applying it to the reddening baton-shaped bruise across Horse's back, Justine arrives in with the news that Schreiner has just been arrested.

"We were down in the *Krug*," she says, "and suddenly these Bullen barge in and one of them tells Adorno that if he doesn't close the place and have it empty within two minutes they'd do it for him. They said someone had set a builder's wagon on fire and had been seen running in there. Adorno said that was rubbish, that it was him who'd actually called the fire brigade. The Bullen left but said they'd be back. People were calling them arseholes and pigs as they went out the door. But they kept their word. A minute later they shot a teargas canister through the door and were wading in with their batons, screaming at us to get out, and calling us dirty communist lefty bastards."

"It's fairly well known as an SPD Kneipe," Our Hero informs them. "A lefty one."

"They arrested a few people but just told the rest of us to disappear. They dragged one woman out by the hair. Schreiner was with us on the other side of the street shouting at them. He still had a bottle of that really strong beer in his hand. Trust him to have held onto it. He was really getting worked up and out of it and finally chucked the bottle at one of the transits, but before it even hit the thing two Zivis - they'd been standing beside us all the time - had him on the ground and were calling out to the uniformed ones for help. There was nothing we could do, except run."

"Scheiße," Our Hero says. "I hope the fuck he's still not on probation."

Tina and Joschka are facing each other, lying on their sides. His larger hips are between her legs and he's moving his cock gently in and out of her, his hands on her breasts. She's closed her eyes and is blacking out everything except his warm sturdy hard-on bringing her gently to orgasm. She begins to move with him, finding his hands, pressing them harder to her breasts hungry for their touch, finding a shared rhythm, forgetting him, herself, everything.

"I'm going to come soon," he whispers.

"Me too, just wait a little."

She moves harder, faster, pushing her clitoris down against his cock.

Melting into each other's juice and sweat, she comes first, he shortly afterwards, and they sprawl on the mattress, the sun flowing through the windows onto their exhausted rejuvenated bodies.

They are gentler with each other then, kissing each other tenderly, caressing each other with a new-found playfulness.

This is the best time, she thinks.

"It's really good not to have to worry about getting pregnant," she says after a while. "It's just so much easier to let go."

"I'm glad."

She'd had a coil fitted a few days earlier.

Eventually they get up. It's still morning. They have the whole warm day in front of them.

"These are all only first names," Porsche says, looking through the sheets of notes he has taken. "We need family names for proper identification. If you can't provide them, you'll have to go through our mug shots. I'm sure we have most of them on file - at HQ."

To be seen anywhere near a police building is the last thing his informant wants. Meeting Porsche here in this Kantstraße apartment, obviously rented out especially for these kinds of liaisons is risky enough.

"It's difficult to get family names. We don't use them. The only way I can do it is from letters or being nosey. Someone might get suspicious."

Porsche notes the 'we'.

Even after years of processing informants in the Political Department, he finds their weird loyalties, if they could be called loyalties, still intrigue him.

"There are ways in which you can make yourself - shall we say - unsuspicious."

"I know."

"We had a little chat about it the time before last. Or has the cat got your memory?"

"You also said that there are limits to how far one can go."

"But they are flexible. Depending on the situation, of course." And then, in quite a different tone, as if it were off the record: "And how far did you go last Saturday anyway?"

"I set the barricade on fire."

The blatancy of the admission is three-pronged: I hate you bastards and I have the guts to do something about it! And I dare you to do something about that! It catches Porsche slightly off guard and that annoys him.

"By yourself?"

"Yes, but someone would have done it anyway."

"Nobody ever gave you permission to initiate criminal acts. My instructions have been quite clear. You may participate passively, but not initiate or take an active part. You know damn well that's just not on!"

He believes he really believes that. He has no authority to process agents provocateurs and he probably would have qualms about it if he was asked to, though he probably would. But then, the borderline was hazy sometimes.

"We could do you for that," he adds.

"But you won't! And besides the only proof you have is this conversation ..."

"Don't be cheeky!" Porsche cuts him short. But the bastard is right of course. After a while the blackmail becomes mutual.

"Who built the barricade?"

"About twenty people. Most of them were masked."

"Did you recognise any of them?"

"They were masked."

"And the ones who weren't - did you recognise any of them?"

"Two of them were foreigners."

"Foreigners?"

"Yes, they spoke with accents."

"God, you are a fount of information. What kinds of accents were they? Turkish, Italian, Chinese, Russian? And when they weren't speaking German, what did they speak?"

"English."

"That's better. And now could you please describe these people to me?"

Trouble is, Porsche muses, as he notes down the descriptions, you never know when these little bits and pieces were going to be useful. But some day some of it would be. In fact, he has no doubt at all that some of these people are potential terrorists.

"And what about the others - the Germans who didn't wear masks?

His informant is silent.

"You know some of them, don't you'?"

"One."

That's probably a lie, Porsche thinks. Those divided loyalties again.

"Name?"

"Joschka."

"The same Joschka we spoke about. Earlier."

"Yes."

It isn't evidence of course, but it would go into the computer. Its time of usefulness would come.

"Are you sure you don't know the names of any of the others?"

"Yes."

Porsche decides to call it a day.

"Okay, I hope all this is correct. For your sake! If

you're holding back on us or making up fairy tales, you're the one who's going to suffer for it in the end. And, as I said before, no more initiating actions, only passive participation, and that no more enthusiastically than absolutely necessary. That's a bit of friendly advice, I hope you heed it. I know you are basically the same as them and that if we didn't have this little thing on you, you'd be out there with them. But I'm sure you'll remember which side your bread is buttered on."

From his informant's surly silence Porsche knows he's hit the right nerve.

It's time for the payoff.

Porsche extracts a roll of high-denomination D-Marks.

"Sign here," he says, passing his informant a receipt slip and a biro.

His informant counts the notes.

"I suppose a copy of this receipt is out of the question?" he says, signing.

"You suppose correctly."

14

"You're different," Our Hero tells Mondbogen softly.

He's lying on his back on the carpet. She's sitting cross-legged beside him. Neither are wearing any clothes.

"Everyone is different."

She smiles - her polite inscrutable Chinese one, not her transparent American one, he thinks.

"You waste your sexual energy," she says. "Coming is not the most important thing."

He's more than a mite taken aback by the statement.

"It's life energy, sperm is life energy," she says. "You should use the energy to reach a higher consciousness, not dissipate it."

"And that's bona fide ancient Chinese wisdom, I suppose."

"It is," she laughs. "But you believe what you want to believe."

He reaches out and touches her arm, kisses her breast lightly and lays back again.

"And Bhagwan wisdom too?"[63]

"Don't be facetious!"

"I wasn't being."

"I don't know," she says, being serious. "I'm not

---

[63] Reference is to Bhagwan Shree Rajneesh, an Indian guru whose followers wear distinctive orange clothing and a picture of the guru on a necklace around their necks. They are part of the street scene in West Berlin.

Bhagwan and I don't want to be. I like being with them because of the good vibrations I feel when I'm with them. That's all."

He shakes his head.

"Some of the things they are into are okay," he admits. "Like vegetarianism and meditation and therapy maybe. But, for fuck's sake, they way they run around all dressed the same, all of them with exactly the same picture of their ayatollah around their necks ... that's totally fascistic."

"And what about you and your friends. You wear a uniform."

He gives her a genuinely puzzled look.

"Your leather jacket is a uniform. And now you are even talking about dyeing your clothes black."

"That's a ...," he thinks quickly, "... it's an anti-uniform. And besides, we don't have leaders."

"Anti-uniform or not, it still alienates people."

"Yeah, the Bullen and the powers that be. It's meant to."

"And nearly everyone else!"

Welcoming parties meet the first guests who cross the border at Dreilinden and Staaken. There aren't as many as have been hoped for, but it's early days yet. In Wedding there's a torch-lit demo. In Kreuzberg the KuKuCK holds a free concert. It's a basic principle of Tuwat that all events be free.

The music pounds between the walls in the long KuKuCK café. It's packed: pacifists and militants, punks and hippies, 68ers and 81ers. Dancing vibrant bodies hopping with a vengeance. That party smell of sweat, tobacco, hash and alcohol in the clammy evening air.

Justine, at the bar, a plastic cup of white wine in her hand, is beginning to feel the effects of the Lebanese. It's coming in pulses, in time with the music - the drummer is good, and the beat of those bongos - with the movements of the dancers. Silently, she finds herself chanting 'tu-wat do-wat tu-wat' to herself as if it were a mantra. Everything seems to be whirling into a single vortex: the dancing bodies, minds, people, spinning with the planet through the dark starry vacuum of space on its endless journey to God-knows-where, not that He/She/It exists ...

Crazy! Fou! It's strong stuff.

She lights a cigarette - the nicotine will steady her - and watches Mondbogen dancing, her waist-long black hair whirling around her small gyrating body.

Our Hero is looking at Mondbogen too, happy at her, happy at everything right then, feeling in a way that he's perhaps having the time of his life. The right mixture of home-grown and Schultheiß, he tells himself, and laughs inwardly at the typical inappropriateness of his unreal cynicism.

He sees Justine.

"Fantastic atmosphere," he shouts into her ear as he orders another beer.

She nods and shouts back: "Is Tina here?"

"She said she'd be along later. You missed dinner tonight. Mondbogen cooked. Chinese." He takes a slug from his Schultheiß. "You know, it's really good that you moved in. It really is. We all like you."

"Really," she mutters, more than slightly embarrassed, secretly pleased, wondering what on earth she is supposed to say to that. Typical of him to go all mellow and sentimental when he's drunk.

She glimpses Schreiner beyond Mondbogen's swirling hair. He's pissed too by the look of him. Tentatively, with a bottle of beer in one hand and a cigarette in the other, he's beginning to join in the dancing.

Schreiner's aware he's drunk and he's enjoying it. He loves being totally out of it. He recognises one of the dancers - the Chinese-American girl, the one Our Hero seems to have something going with. He catches her eye and she his. Smiles, simple demandless smiles flash between them. He says something to her but by the time she replies in her funny American accent, he's forgotten what he originally said. Jesus Christ, as the Irish were always saying, is he pissed!

"Have you been in this place before?" Our Hero asks Justine.

"A few times," she nods.

"I mean upstairs in the other parts?"

She nods again.

"What's it like?"

"They do a lot of theatre and dance. And they show films sometimes. Obscure and experimental stuff. Not obviously political like in the *Frontkino*. It's used for meetings of the Betsetzer Council. The rooms upstairs are massive. Used to be a factory. They made army uniforms here during the war. The SS headquarters used to be across the road, and you know that weird hotel next door, Himmler apparently used to drink his carrot juice there. He was quite into alternative medicine, homeopathy and all that, herbs ... a pretty weird area this, I wouldn't like to walk around it on acid."

The drums and the bongos start up again ... the present, becomes graspable, no longer a mere prelude to what comes next.

Phew!

She finishes her wine, says she's going to dance and disappears into the throng.

Our Hero finishes his beer and follows her.

Another of the endless pots of filter coffee is put down on the yellow table in the common room, the soundtrack of *A Clockwork Orange* churning over in the cassette player for the umpteenth time.

"I'd heard something about Tuwat," Merton is saying. "Word gets around. But we knew that a lot of squatting was going on in Berlin anyway."

He's just arrived and it's about the third time he's had to explain himself that day. The Tuwat office down the street has given him this address. This time it's to Kalypso and Horse he's explaining.

Joschka is browsing through the latest copy of the *Besetzer Post*. They're all slightly stoned - with the exception of Kalypso.

Merton pours them some more of the duty-free Cointreau he picked up transiting East Germany.

"Are there many occupations in England?" Kalypso asks.

Merton is from Brixton.

"Squats. Yes. The peak was a few years ago but it's picking up again now. People tend to keep quiet about it. They don't hang banners out the windows advertising the fact. It's not so openly political as here. People do it mainly to get a roof over their heads, but that's pretty political, I guess."

"That's the reason I did it," she says. "To get a roof over mine and Fröschchen's head."

"Fröschchen?"

"My small daughter."

Merton nods. Culture shock and hitching from London, with a quick stopover in Amsterdam, had played havoc with his biorhythms. But since he's been here things have simply fallen into place. All part of the divine plan, no doubt.

The Beethoven Ninth track comes on.

"I thought it'd be more or less like the London scene," Horse informs him.

"What's the main difference?"

"The attitude really, I suppose," Horse says, rolling another joint from the freshly steam-dried home-grown. "Take this!" He indicates the pile of grass. "People here seem more to regard it as their right to smoke the stuff. They do it openly, more up front, not behind the bike shed like naughty boys - or girls. Like the way it is in Dublin. But it's other things too. Like the other day when the local gutter press started going on about how the squatters were being financed from Moscow - you know, the usual shite - a gang of them went down to the local Soviet Consulate or whatever they have here and demanded that they be given all these roubles they were supposed to be getting - creating a bit of an international incident. They got fuck all roubles, but it was a good laugh!"

He lets out one of his long loud laughs before going on.

"Seriously though, I spent some time in a squat in Camden last summer and the apathy there was fucking chronic. Here, when the pigs evict a house there's a fucking riot. It makes the bastards think twice. But then the laws here are different. The cops here can more or less evict you whenever they feel like it. There's no fucking around wasting time going getting eviction orders and that shite. If they want to search a place they don't even need a warrant. Bit like in Ireland. Which explains why there's fuck all squatting there. That's my impression anyway."

Merton notices that the white kitchen wall is covered with graffiti: German, English, French, other European languages he doesn't recognise - and even some that looks like Chinese or Japanese.

"The best squatting - on a large scale - I've come across is in Denmark, at Christiana," he says.

"Yes, I have heard about that," Joschka says, suddenly interested.

"It's big," Merton says. "They call it a Free Town, which it is in a way. It's an old naval base right in the middle of Copenhagen. People moved in there in the early 70s and it's been going strong ever since. A good few hundred people live there all year round. They have all sorts of things: a bicycle factory run as a collective that actually builds bicycles more or less from scratch, a bakery, an alternative health centre, a communal sauna, a candle factory, a theatre, a place where they restore and build wood stoves, a workshop where you can build your own windmill and the biggest hash market in Europe. They even have some farmland. Last time I was there I saw this woman taking a shower in the altogether ..."

"The altogether?" Joschka asks.

" ... in the nude, naked," Merton explains, "right out

in the open, on the street – if you can call it a street, there're no cars. And nobody hassled her and she knew nobody would. That's pretty civilised in my book. Know what I mean, like?"

"From what I heard," Horse says, "it can be a fucking heavy place too."

Merton's a few years older than them and wears his long hair in a ponytail. He's wondering if they're thinking he's a sentimental old hippy.

"It can be. But mainly around the hash market. That's just inside the entrance and it's only a fraction of the total area. Once you get beyond that, it's fine. A lot of the heaviness has to do with smack coming into the place recently."

"Smack?" Joschka asks.

"Heroin, junk," Merton says. "Where there's an overworld there's an underworld. You can't really get rid of it, all you can do is contain it. Last I heard they were trying to get the heroin dealers out of the place. I'm sure you have it here in some of the houses too - it's inevitable if you live outside the law in this way. Squats, by their very nature, are refuges for all sorts of people."

"That is what happened to the AJZ, the autonomous youth centre in Zurich," Joschka adds. "After spending a year fighting the police on the streets to keep it open, the people there decided to close it down themselves. There was too much heroin, too many junkies making everything kaput. It would not surprise me if the state had something to do with it. I have read that that kind of thing - putting heroin into a scene to destroy it - has been done in Italy and in America."

"Nah," Horse shakes his head, and takes a first toke on the joint. "No need to. People like smack and it'll turn up whenever the law isn't around. You're too paranoid. Smack's just a scapegoat. Make the box illegal and the norms would be out there mugging pensioners to get their nightly fix of *Coronation Street*. It's not the state that's strong, it's the people that are weak."

"You underestimate the amount of evil people there are in the world," Kalypso said quietly, "hidden away in positions of power."

"Evil. Good," Horse says. "Out-dated concepts. Just like optimism and pessimism. People just occupy different head spaces."

Merton is interested in how the squatting in Berlin started.

"Read this," Horse hands him a copy of the Magazine. The cover is a drawing of a fag-smoking Berlin bear in a dirty mac flashing, his genitals blacked out. "There's an interview on the centre spread that's fairly informative – if you read between the lines."

"It started last November," Joschka says. "A prisoner support group from Libertäres Forum, a kind of anarchist group, occupied the Besetzer-Eck - that's a house in another part of Kreuzberg - so that people coming out of prison would have somewhere to go. They did it during a demonstration - they went into the house and put banners up while the demonstration was passing. The first fighting with the police was in December. They were totally confused at first, about the whole situation. That was obvious from just listening to their radio. After that the movement really took off."

"This has been a special summer," Kalypso elaborates. "Last year there was nothing - no squatted houses, no demos, no riots."

"Yeah," Joschka agrees. "The air around here has never been freer."

Merton nods. Maybe the fact that the city is surrounded by the Wall means that energy doesn't become as dissipated as it does in London.

Kalypso and Tina are on the roof. The afternoon sun is baking. Tina has taken refuge in the shade of the chimney stack.

"Deciding to have Fröschchen was such a long-term commitment," Kalypso is saying, her light summer shorts draping her eyes from the sun, "that I had to really think about my priorities."

Tina always has to think for a second when Kalypso says 'Fröschchen' rather than 'my baby' or 'my child'. For her a baby is a baby like any other, nameless. She looks again at Kalypso's tanned nursing breasts.

"It put things into a different perspective for me," Kalypso goes on. "I left school at sixteen and my family is old Berlin working class. My father died when I was a kid and my mother worked behind a bar in a grotty Kneipe for years. When I left home I spent a lot of time pissing around, not knowing where I was going. Some of the scenes I got involved in were fairly kaput. Then one bright day I found out I was going to be a single unemployed mother – every social worker's wet dream - and woke up. I never really even thought about an abortion. If I was going to rear Fröschchen and have a future I had to get things together quickly and develop the habit of keeping myself together. In fact, I first became involved in this political stuff when I was pregnant."

Tina feels that she's too together, too much a child of the post-war Federal Republic middle-class Wirtschaftswunder, too shaped by the certainties and smugness of the Catholic village where she grew up. She doesn't seem to have that capacity for living in the moment she sees in Ursula and Justine – and Horse.

And Kalypso does appear bien dans sa peau[64] - as Justine would put it. Having Fröschchen certainly has something to do with it. But the idea of a woman being fulfilled by a child ...

In the distance, on the Other Side, the revolving orb on the top of the East Berlin television tower glitters in the sun. The outline of the cross the sun's reflection inadvertently makes on it is one of those standing anti-DDR jokes. And, like most of them, not that funny.

She begins to roll a cigarette.

"How come you moved into this house?" Kalypso asks.

Tina tells her, more or less. Going into why she had left the uni sounds hollow.

"Sometimes I think the politics of this whole thing are a bit dubious," Kalypso says. "Like the Chamissoplatz riot. I mean, was that really necessary? A lot of macho posing if you ask me. On both sides. Getting a place to live and all that is fine and good, but there's a lot of other stuff that strikes me as being ... patriarchal shit?"

---

[64] Literally: 'well in one's skin', French.

Down in the courtyard a conversation is taking place. They can hear each word crystal clear as it echoes upwards.

Horse is slouched in one of the armchairs, smoking the last of the home-grown. Ancient images of white Russian snow and grey armies pummelling each other mercilessly are flashing across the TV screen to the tune of the *UB40* tape in the cassette player. He guesses it's an East German channel. West German TV doesn't seem to have the same propensity for displaying the embarrassing past. "And TV is called escaping from reality," he mutters to himself.

The knock on the door ignites a familiar flash of paranoia.

But it's only Wilde.

"Just passing and I thought I'd drop in," he says, easing himself into one of the armchairs.

"How are things?" Horse asks.

"Been involved in getting a few things organised for Tuwat."

"Any particular wishes in the tea department? We've got that green Gun Powder stuff. Scouts honour, I won't spike it."

"Dockers'. Strong, milk and two sugar."

"When I makes tee I makes tee – and when I makes water I makes water. As Mother Joyce would say."

Horse finds some Aldi teabags.

"I've been considering heading back to the old sod," he says. It's something he's been thinking about but hasn't mentioned to anyone. "Mother fucking Ireland and all that."

"Any particular reason?"

"Boredom maybe. It's hard to get involved in things when you've keine Deutsch. People get tired of talking to me in English all the time. Not that I blame them."[65]

"You could learn German."

"Not motivated enough. Heard you got beaten up a while back!"

"Heard something similar about you," Wilde replies.

Horse made one of his that's-life faces.

"Occupational hazard, I suppose", Wilde shrugs. "Maybe I'm getting too old for the game."

"Or your luck's running out," Horse suggests. "It scared the fucking shit out of me. Violence is not all it's made out to be. If that cop had aimed a few inches higher I'd have ended up with a cracked skull."

"Maybe I've lost my nerve," Wilde adds.

"Nature of fear, isn't it! And that's what they want to do basically. Scare the living daylights out of you!"

"Makes you think though," Wilde said.

"Not if they crack your skull."

"Oh, just about the whole point of taking them on like that - physically, I mean. A lot of people have been hurt, most of them people who were just standing around, and far more of us than them. And next month is not going to be a picnic either, what with these evictions coming up and Mister Haig coming to pay us a visit."

"You don't really believe in the innocent civilians lark, do you?" says Horse. "People should have

[65] keine Deutsch - no German.

enough cop by now to realise that if they hang around the place while there's a riot going on, they're not innocent bystanders, they're water for the fish."

"That's what Napoleon Bonaparte Lummer says."

"And he's right."

"It's not as simple as that."

Horse decides not to argue the point. He's been having too many pointless arguments lately.

"And what have you being organising for the révolutionette?"

"Tuwat?"

"What else?"

"An exhibition to be shown in the *Chamisso Galerie* and later in the KuKuCK. And a series of discussions about prisons to be held in the Tenants Centre. We're trying to get a film from West Germany on El Salvador for the *Frontkino*."

Horse nods, impressed.

"You been one of these people handing out leaflets inviting people to free high German teas in the exclusive *Kempenskis* on the Ku'damn?"

"Afraid not!"

Wilde's gradually getting to like this guy. But he has to get a move on.

"Thanks for the dockers'."

"The pleasure's mine, sir."

15

At Platz der Luftbrücke the multicoloured crowd is gathering once again. This time in front of USAF Templehof. The monumental relic of Nazi splendour, Leggo-like, towers above the banners and the flags – the red and the black and all the other colours of the rainbow. The usual crazy crowd, though there are more in tattered black leather jackets today - despite the heat. And, of course, the Bullen are there too, sweating in their olive-green overalls and plastic helmets, as impatient as anyone else for things to get going.

Which it does, suddenly. First, in dribs and drabs, then in a torrent, down Mehringdamn, towards Yorckstraße, the route we've trodden so many times in joyous and defiant pilgrimage, the music blaring.

without a break for breath

It's hot. A day to wander naked in the sun, one or two people think at same time. So off they come, the black drainpipe trousers, the T-shirts and leather jackets - and male vultures in the form of press photographers close in on the stripping Punks. All those tits and bums - for free - in broad daylight - on the public street - are positively irresistible.

One of the Punk girls gives them the finger.

"Piss off you fucking arseholes!" she screams.

They snap that too. A naked sixteen-year-old telling them to fuck off is front-page stuff.

She'd like to shove their expensive equipment up their fucking arses and down the throats of their leering cocker-spaniel gobs. But fuck them, they're not worth the fucking bother.

history is being made
es geht voran!

The urge to strip off spreads, descends at random.

Two guys draw anarchist 'A's and Besetzer signs on each other's buttocks with a felt-tip marker, show their arses to the cameras and cause another flurry of free press activity. This time the *taz* photographer is on the job too, painfully aware that he must look like one of the vultures - and for a moment wonders if he is one of them.

Left at Mehringdamn and then on to good old Yorkstraße.

And leading the way, walkie-talkie in hand, is your friendly neighbourhood Bulle, smiling, bearded, keeping in touch with Zentrale. And enjoying himself too by the look of it.

A few bangers go off here and there. But the sounds of war go against the grain today and are cursed away.

A row of Bullen, forever reminiscent of Roman Legionaries, standing guard outside the Social Welfare Office, are surrounded by dancing naked barbarians. Click, click go the cameras and more than a couple of their stony faces are forced to melt into boyish grins.

Oh, if only all human severity could be made to melt into smiles like that, even embarrassed ones. A dream to be sure but today's as much a day of dreams as any day will ever be, nicht wahr! A day on which latter-day barbarians dance naked around latter-day legionaries.[66]

history is being made
es geht voran!

One prancing happy barbarian, naked except for a

[66] nicht wahr - is that not true?

ski-mask over his hairy head, leather jacket and jeans stuffed in a plastic bag from Aldi's, gym shoes still on though, puts his arm around the neighbourhood Bulle with the walkie-talkie. The cameras home in. The Bulle smiles. Well, even us Polizisten have to smile sometimes, and well it sure beats us beating the shit out of each other, even if my colleagues will never let me live this down.

space labs are falling on islands

Two guys, their pricks tied together with a necktie from God knows where, dance arm in arm down the avenue.

forgetfulness is spreading

The invisible spectre of Carlos Castaneda's Don Juan's Death whispers a reminder of his existence into Our Hero's left ear. He hops onto the grass verge and starts to strip off.[67]

"Come on, liberate yourself," he calls to Horse.

Horse shakes his head and laughs.

es geht voran!

As the human river of colour and music flows by, Our Hero struggles with his denims, T-shirt and skid-marked underpants and wraps them up in his leather jacket.

mountains are exploding

They plunge into the river again.

---

[67] Carlos Castaneda (1925-1998), American author, wrote a series of books featuring a Mexican Yaqui Shaman called Don Juan (possibly fictional). One of Don Juan's teachings was that one's Death was one's ally and should be consulted before all decisions. The books also describe hallucinogenic experiences induced by peyote and various mushrooms, as well as describing methods to induce and control lucid dreams.

the president is guilty

Up ahead the great iron echo chambers, the railway bridges of Yorckstraße loom.

"That's it, fellow human beings, liberate yourselves," Helga Goetze cries, sandwiched between her placards.[68]

The first human wave surges under the cast-iron girders, whooping and howling, playing urban Indians, followed by the second wave and the next and the next, heading towards Potsdamer Straße.

es geht voran!

On a balcony some Teds[69] - caught in a time warp - amuse themselves with obscene gestures at the pretentious fucking masses passing below, but nobody takes any particular notice of them.

grey b-film heroes
are about to rule the world

A flashy white sports car, its polished affluence gleaming, is set on by a gang of Punks armed with spray cans and intent on anti-social no-future devilry. They draw anarchist 'A's all over it and write SCHEIßAUTO on the bonnet.[70]

es geht voran!

"Tut tut," titters another sort of subversive: one plastered in mascara, wearing a leather jacket and, from the waist down, black suspenders and black

---

[68] Helga Sophia Goetze (1922-2008), German artist, poet and political activist. Some of her work can be seen at http://www.helga-goetze.de/html/stickbilder-ubersicht.html.

[69] Teddy Boys - British 1950's subculture, typified by young men wearing clothes partly inspired by Edwardian dandies.

[70] SCHEIßAUTO - shit car.

nylons on his shaved and shapely legs, balancing precariously on a pair of pink stilettos - one of the boys from Tuntenhaus playing his role to a tee.[71]

es geht voran!

Click. Justine captures the image. But she thinks twice about snapping the Punks. They're not wearing masks and might not appreciate her photographie engagée. Instead she turns to the three Anatolians, grey suited, moustached and bellied, standing in front of a kebab takeaway watching the mad Deutsche world pass by.

"What, are you protesting against?" a well-meaning citizen asks a mild-looking Punk.

"Against everything," she replies smiling. "Everything!"

[71] Tuntenhaus - queer house.

Postscript

On September 15 Alexander Haig, the US Secretary of State, visited Berlin and spoke to the Senate. About 80,000 people demonstrated against his presence and there was fierce rioting. On September 22 the nine houses were evicted. While Innensenator Lummer was giving a post-eviction victory press conference and having himself photographed on the balcony of one of the evicted houses, a group of people gathered outside to protest. The police chased the crowd onto the busy Potsdamer Straße where a young West German, the nineteen year-old Claus-Jürgen Rattay, was hit by a bus and dragged along the street and killed. This was followed by all-night rioting and for several days the spot where he died became a place of pilgrimage, a place to put flowers.

'Our weapons are words, and we may need our arsenal at any moment. *Don Quixote* is always at my side … *Don Quixote* is the best book of political theory.'
- Zapatista Subcomandante Marcos, 2001

Some weapons:

Anarchism : A History Of Libertarian Ideas and Movements, George Woodcock
A PDF of this book is available here:
http://libcom.org/library

Anarchy in Action, Colin Ward
http://en.wikipedia.org/wiki/Colin_Ward

Down Wind of Eden, Tom Chektout, Hooligan Press 1988

Fields, Factories and Workshops: or Industry Combined with Agriculture and Brain Work with Manual Work
Peter Kropotkin
PDF and range of ebook versions here:
http://archive.org/details/cu31924032409710
See also http://en.wikipedia.org/wiki/Kropotkin

Fragments of an Anarchist Anthropology by David Graeber
PDF version available here: http://www.prickly-paradigm.com/sites/default/files/Graeber_PPP_14_0.pdf

Homage to Catalonia, George Orwell
http://en.wikipedia.org/wiki/Homage_to_Catalonia

Squatting in West Berlin, Hooligan Press, 1987

The Soul of Man Under Socialism, Oscar Wilde
http://en.wikipedia.org/wiki/
The_Soul_of_Man_under_Socialism

Rick Roderick's *a psychological exposition for upbuilding and awakening*, 3 courses
on historical developments within Western philosophy
from a fairly anarchist perspective.
All 24 video-lectures be downloaded here:
http://rickroderick.org/

Voltairine de Cleyre, her poetry and essays
http://voltairine.org/
http://en.wikipedia.org/wiki/Voltairine_de_Cleyre

Wikipedia articles on Anarchism and Squatting:
http://en.wikipedia.org/wiki/Anarchism
http://en.wikipedia.org/wiki/Squatting

ALSO FROM HOOLIGAN PRESS/CAMBRIA BOOKS

DOC CHAOS: The Chernobyl Effect & The Last Laugh by David Thorpe

Inside a nuclear reactor, no one can hear you scream - with pleasure.

"DOC CHAOS is one of the most exciting and refreshing pieces of graphic literature I've seen in a long time." - *Alan Moore.*

Doc Chaos, the scientific prodigy who sold the promise of nuclear power to the most gullible, power-mad people in the world - politicians - did so not just because he likes seeing humanity "trip on its own banana skins" (Graeme Basset), but for a much darker, more erotic reason... to reach the ultimate climax.

This new edition of the ground-breaking novella by David Thorpe, author of the award-winning novel Hybrids, contains 12 illustrations by prominent stars of the comics art world: Simon Bisley ~ Brian Bolland ~ Brett Ewins ~ Duncan Fegredo ~ Rian Hughes ~ Lin Jammett ~ Pete Mastin ~ Dave McKean ~ Savage Pencil ~ Ed Pinsent ~ Bryan Talbot.

It also contains a new short story, The Last Laugh, culminating the Doc Chaos narrative at the coming apocalypse, and a new Afterword by the Author, which sets the two pieces in their creative context.

DOC CHAOS takes the literary genealogy of doctors Frankenstein, Faustroll and Benway into the nuclear age and beyond. A love story, that makes Fifty Shades of Grey look like kindergarten games ...

"No one could be fully prepared for DOC CHAOS. This is a comedy of terrors." - *Don Watson, NME.*

"A hugely entertaining book, full of humour, satire, and an appealing, idiosyncratic perception of the way things are." - *Dale Luciano, the Comics Journal.*

"The creators of DOC CHAOS face up to the unbridled crap which is threatening our existence. DOC CHAOS hopes the forces of authority will slip on their own banana skins. Fast-moving and funny."
- Graeme Basset, Infinity.

Price: £1.84. Available on Amazon for the Kindle at
www.amazon.co.uk/dp/B008PYLRXM/ref=rdr_kindle_ext_tmb
or at www.davidthorpe.info/bookshop.htm for other formats.

Lightning Source UK Ltd.
Milton Keynes UK
UKHW021016200820
368550UK00018B/2307